"I Have A Proposal For You."

He leaned against the counter like a lazy puma. "How romantic."

"Not that kind of proposal." Her voice had a prim, school-mistressy snap that she instantly regretted. "A…business proposition."

"Perhaps we should go somewhere more private." His dark eyes added an undercurrent of suggestion to his words. He turned his head to the hotel clerk. "She won't be needing her room."

A surge of desire, tangled up with fear and anticipation and even—already—regret for what she was about to do, rose through her body like a flash flood. She lifted her bag higher on her shoulder. She was strong now. She could handle him. She'd have to.

"Why won't I need my room?" The question was purely for show, since they both knew the answer.

"You'll be staying with me. Just like old times."

Dear Reader,

I had always heard that the history of South Florida did not go back much past the invention of air-conditioning. When I moved here last year, I was surprised and excited to discover a tangled web of history involving conquistadors, pirates, Seminole indians, soldiers, tycoons and adventurers.

Hurricanes are a familiar aspect of life in South Florida, and I soon learned about the large number of shipwrecks off the coast, dating back to the early Spanish treasure fleets. Excavation is under way right now on several vessels, with probably the most well known being Mel Fisher's recovery of the *Nuestra Señora de Atocha,* with its huge stash of gold coins and silver ingots.

I began to imagine a hero who searches the seas for treasure. And what if my hero was the descendant of a pirate, whose ship had sunk with his ill-gotten gains? Throw in a feisty heroine determined never to fall for the hero again and it sounded like a brew as salty and tangy as a frozen margarita. I had a blast writing this tale, and I hope you enjoy Jack and Vicki's story!

All the best,

Jennifer Lewis

JENNIFER LEWIS

THE DEEPER THE PASSION...

HARLEQUIN®
entertain, enrich, inspire™

Recycling programs
for this product may
not exist in your area.

ISBN-13: 978-0-373-73215-9

THE DEEPER THE PASSION...

www.Harlequin.com

Printed in U.S.A.

Books by Jennifer Lewis

Harlequin Desire

†*The Prince's Pregnant Bride* #2082
†*At His Majesty's Convenience* #2094
†*Claiming His Royal Heir* #2105
 Behind Boardroom Doors #2144
** *The Cinderella Act* #2170
** *The Deeper the Passion...* #2202

Silhouette Desire

 The Boss's Demand #1812
 Seduced for the Inheritance #1830
 Black Sheep Billionaire #1847
 Prince of Midtown #1891
* *Millionaire's Secret Seduction* #1925
* *In the Argentine's Bed* #1931
* *The Heir's Scandalous Affair* #1938
 The Maverick's Virgin Mistress #1977
 The Desert Prince #1993
 Bachelor's Bought Bride #2012

*The Hardcastle Progeny
†Royal Rebels
**The Drummond Vow

Other titles by this author available in ebook format.

JENNIFER LEWIS

has been dreaming up stories for as long as she can remember and is thrilled to be able to share them with readers. She has lived on both sides of the Atlantic and worked in media and the arts before she grew bold enough to put pen to paper. She would love to hear from readers at jen@jenlewis.com. Visit her website at www.jenlewis.com.

One

"It's pronounced *sin-cere*." Vicki St. Cyr leaned on the hotel counter. She was used to having her name mangled.

"Don't believe a word of it." The deep, rich voice in her ear made her start and spin around. Those familiar flashing dark eyes were settled firmly on the hotel clerk. "She's not to be trusted at all."

The young female behind the desk looked up, and her face took on that foolish sparkle of a girl suddenly confronted with the attentions of a handsome predatory male. "Can I help you, sir?"

"I'll let you know." Jack looked back at Vicki, and she felt her blood heat.

"Hi, Jack." Vicki realized, too late, that she'd crossed her arms defensively over her chest. "Fancy seeing you here."

"Vicki, what a surprise." His voice contained no more astonishment than hers. His gaze seemed to peer right through her carefully groomed exterior and flay bare a small part of her soul. If she still had a soul. "I hear you're looking for me."

She swallowed. How had he heard? She'd hoped at least for the advantage of surprise. But then Jack had always been two strides ahead of her. Why would now be any different? "I have a proposal for you."

He leaned against the counter like a lazy puma. "How romantic."

"Not that kind of proposal." Her voice had a prim, schoolmistressy snap that she instantly regretted. "A... business proposition."

"Perhaps we should go somewhere more private." His dark eyes added an undercurrent of suggestion to his words. He turned his head to the clerk. "She won't be needing her room."

A surge of desire, tangled up with fear and anticipation and even—already—regret for what she was about to do, rose through her body like a flash flood. She lifted her bag higher on her shoulder. She was strong now. She could handle him. She'd have to.

"Why won't I need my room?" The question was purely for show because they both knew the answer.

"You'll be staying with me. Just like old times." His broad, sensual mouth widened, like the habitual slight grin of a crocodile. He grabbed her bag off the floor and strode for the door. Vicki's faithless eyes tracked his tight behind, clad in faded denim, and the way his worn T-shirt hugged the thick muscle of his back.

"Should I cancel the room?" The desk clerk didn't take her eyes off him, even after he disappeared through the revolving door. "There will be a cancellation charge of fifty dollars because it's already—"

"Yes." Vicki put her credit card on the counter. What was another fifty on top of what she already owed? It would save a fortune over staying in this expensive boutique hotel. Two years of trying to "keep up appearances" had left her close to beggary. Lord knows she wouldn't be here otherwise.

But desperate times called for desperate measures, like daring to set foot in Jack Drummond's lair.

Jack was behind the wheel of his vintage Mustang when she got outside. The fierce South Florida sun beat down on the tarmac and threw dazzling diamond reflections off the custom jade-green paint job. The engine was already running and the passenger door open for her to get in. Did he know she didn't have a car? In the old days she'd have rented one and insisted on driving it just to keep the escape hatch open. Right now she didn't have that luxury. She climbed in and settled herself against the soft leather seat. "How did you know I'd be here?"

"My spies are everywhere." He didn't look at her as he pulled out of the parking lot and left the exclusive Ramona Beach Inn behind.

"You don't have any spies." She seized the opportunity to study his face. Skin tanned to a rich copper as usual, dark hair flecked with gold. "You've always been a one-man band."

"You've been hanging around the New York Drummonds." He still didn't turn toward her, but she saw the muscles tighten in his hand on the wheel. "Figured I was next."

Vicki drew in a breath. "I spent a relaxing few weeks with Sinclair and his mom. It was fun to catch up with old friends."

A smile twitched at the edge of his mouth. "You always have an ulterior motive. The fun is in figuring it out."

She stiffened. "My motives are very simple. I'm helping Katherine Drummond locate the pieces of a three-hundred-year-old family chalice."

"And you're doing this because of your passion for history?" This time he did turn to her. His smile deepened, beneath his bold cheekbones. "I heard you became an antiques dealer."

"The chalice has an interesting story."

"Oh, yes." His voice deepened into a throaty narrator's drone. "Three brothers, tossed by the stormy seas on their passage from bonnie Scotland, bid goodbye to each other in the New World but pledged one day to reunite their family treasure. Only then could the mighty Drummond clan regain the luck of their esteemed ancestors." He tossed a mighty laugh out onto the wind. "Come on, Vicki. That's not your style."

"There's a reward." Might as well come clean. Jack was more likely to be tempted by money than sentiment.

"Ten thousand dollars." He turned off the main road onto an unmarked and unpaved side road, fringed by spiky palms and tall scrub pines. "I've got junk worth more than that in the trunk of my car."

"It's twenty thousand per piece. I convinced Katherine to raise it. To attract the right sort of treasure hunters."

"Like me."

"Like me." She was gratified when he turned to look

at her. His dark gaze met hers and a jolt of emotion leaped through her. Old feelings, long buried, started clawing their way to the surface. She felt a shimmer of panic. "Not that I really need the money, of course. But if I'm going to look for an old cup, there might as well be a profit in it."

"And you need my treasure hunting expertise to claim the reward."

"You're the most successful treasure hunter on the Atlantic coast. I read an article about your new boat and all its expensive equipment. You're famous."

"Some would say notorious."

"And most likely the cup fragment is somewhere in your house." She'd found the first piece in the attic of his cousin Sinclair's Long Island mansion.

"If it's anywhere at all." His hand slid on the wheel as he turned down another unmarked road. The pines and saw palmettos ended as abruptly as the road, which descended suddenly to a beach. Jack swung the car to the left and parked near a broad wooden dock. A good-size boat, white with gleaming chrome rails, bobbed at the far end.

"Your dock looks different than I remember."

"It's been a long time." He was already out of the car and carrying her bag down the dock with feline grace.

"Not that long. There was a building here and a gate." And a bench where they'd once made love under a bright full moon.

"Gone in the last hurricane. Road keeps getting shorter, too."

"Must be frustrating to lose expensive real estate to the sea."

"Not if you enjoy change." He swung her bag into

the boat and turned to watch as she walked along the wood jetty. She hoped her own walk had a fraction of the swagger she admired in his.

He helped her onto his boat, where he'd already slung her bag. She walked around the deck to where a big, padded fighting chair held a commanding position. She perched herself on the seat and grabbed hold of the armrests. Jack had never been a slow driver. The boat lurched to a start and the propeller wash foamed beneath her feet as the engines roared into action. She braced her feet against the footrest as they leaped and bounced over the choppy water. Within a minute or so, Jack's island appeared over the horizon. Fringed with palms, no building visible, it looked like the kind of place you could get marooned and die. And she was going to be trapped here with Jack Drummond, unless she geared herself up for a long and bracing swim.

The dock on the island looked the same as the last time she saw it, years ago. Built of coral rock and carved in the elaborate style of some ancient and wealthy Drummond ancestors, it was flanked with two stone turrets that probably once concealed armed men. Maybe they still did, if tales of Jack's wealth were to be believed.

"Lost your sea legs?" Jack grabbed her arm when she wobbled while trying to climb out of the boat.

"I haven't spent much time on the water lately."

"Shame." His gaze hovered on her face and, to her horror, she felt her skin heat. How did he have this effect on her? She was the one who ate men for breakfast. He was just some scurvy sea dog from her past.

Does he still think I'm beautiful? The sudden thought stabbed her—a pang of insecurity.

Who cares? You're not here to make him fall in love with you. You need his help to find the cup and then you can wash your hands of him forever.

The old house on the island was obviously built more as a fort than a cozy residence. Limestone walls rose from behind the wild hedge of round-leaved sea grape that separated the pale strip of beach from the interior of the island. Only two tiny windows pierced the stone block exterior, although the iron-studded doors were thrown open to let in the morning sun.

"Is there anyone else visiting you?" The open door shoved unwelcome thoughts into her brain. Another woman? She hadn't dared to assume he was single. He never was for long. Women swarmed Jack Drummond like sharks to a flesh wound.

"We'll be alone." He strode ahead of her, sunlight picking out golden highlights in his dark hair. Shadow cloaked him as he entered the tall arched doorway into his private sanctum.

Good. She didn't need competition at this stage. It would be embarrassing flirting in front of someone else. Trying to compete. She might have enjoyed that in the old days, but she didn't have the brash confidence of raw youth anymore.

The intricate colored-marble floor of the entrance hall stood in lush contrast to the fortress exterior. Jack's ancestors may have been pirates, but they also loved beautiful things—expensive things—which might explain why they became pirates in the first place.

Jack looked as arrogant as ever. Even from behind he radiated self-assurance, his broad shoulders set easy against his powerful neck, his hair—too long, as usual—curling almost to the collar of his T-shirt. Jack didn't bother to conform to norms of fashion or try to fit in. He didn't need to. Born into a semicriminal dynasty of treasure hunters, he'd excelled in the family trade and made more money—legally—in the past five years than all his ancestors put together.

He filled a glass of water at the monstrous steel fridge and turned to her, offering it. "Too early in the day for champagne, but I'm celebrating your arrival all the same."

The twinkle in his eye disarmed her as she took the water. Was he really happy to see her? "The pleasure is mutual." She raised her glass of water. Let the flirting begin. "I've missed you, Jack."

"This is getting better every minute. I still can't figure out what you're after."

She smarted under his unromantic retort. He leaned against the broad pine table in the kitchen and crossed his powerful arms. Tiny golden hairs stood out against thick, bronzed muscle. She cursed herself for noticing.

"Isn't it enough to visit one old friend while helping out another?"

"Nope. And half of a twenty-thousand-dollar reward isn't enough to tempt the Vicki St. Cyr I know. Unless your financial situation has changed." His eyes narrowed slightly, and she felt their dark perceptive power.

She swallowed and stiffened but tried not to show her anxiety. The press hadn't yet sniffed out her father's sudden descent into financial ruin. The confusion created by his death from a stroke had provided a smokescreen. Her mom had slipped off to Corsica with a wealthy friend of her dad, and the only person left holding the empty bag was her.

"I can always find something pretty to spend ten

thousand dollars on." She played with her silver brace-
let, which was probably worth about twelve dollars. "It's
a curse to be raised with expensive tastes."

"Unless you're born gagging on a silver spoon.
You've never needed to make money."

"I find it emotionally satisfying." If Jack knew she
truly needed the money he'd be less likely to help her.
He'd be unable to fight the urge to play with her, like a
cat with a trapped mouse. "It makes me feel normal."

Jack threw his head back, and a great guffaw filled
the kitchen, bounced off the stone surfaces of the walls
and floor and echoed off the high ceiling. "Normal?
You're probably the least normal person I know, and
that's why I enjoy you so much."

"It's been a long time, Jack. Perhaps I'm more con-
ventional than I used to be."

"I doubt it." A tiny smile pulled at one corner of his
mouth.

"Why do *you* bother to make money?" Going on
the offensive might be her best line of defense. "You
could have lived comfortably on the ill-gotten gains of
your ancestors, but instead you're out there every day
trawling the oceans for gold doubloons as if your life
depended on it."

"I get bored easily."

Vicki's stomach clenched. He'd grown bored with
her. Eight magical months, then one day he was gone,
off to pursue more elusive treasure and find a new damsel for his bed. "So you do. And what do you do with
all the money you make?"

"Some of it I spend on new toys, the rest I just keep
lying around the house in sacks." Mischief twinkled
again in his eyes, which stayed firmly fixed on her.

She fought a sudden urge to scan the place for burlap bags filled with Spanish silver. "I have expensive taste in boats, especially my newest."

"I'd like to see it."

"Her." Mischief sparkled in his eyes again.

Vicki tensed as visions of a hard-bodied blonde crept into her mind. "Oh, your boat is female."

"They all are."

"Why is that?"

He shrugged. "Maybe because they drive us men crazy." His gaze lingered on her face, and she felt her skin heat. "But we love them anyway."

The word *love* made her jump slightly. Not a real jump, a jolt deep inside her. Either way, it made her feel even more off kilter than she did already. How did Jack Drummond manage to fluster her like no other man?

"So, this cup. It's part of your family history and probably stowed in a dusty corner of this old pile." She gestured at the stone walls around them. "Any idea where it is?"

Jack tilted his head slightly as if thinking. "No idea at all."

"Can we search your family records?"

"Pirates aren't known for keeping detailed records. It's harder to deny having stuff that's written down."

"People don't get as rich as your ancestors by being loosey-goosey with the books." She lifted a thoughtful finger to her lips. "I bet there are some old leather-bound ledgers somewhere."

"Even if there were, why would they bother to cat-alog a worthless old cup piece? They probably threw it away."

"A family heirloom? I think not." Though a shiver of

apprehension did cool her. People threw away priceless things every day because they didn't look like the stuff on department store shelves. "The Drummonds are far too proud of their auld Scottish ancestry for that. Look." She pointed at the old stone kitchen fireplace. Above the big opening where cauldrons once boiled was a big crest, its paint faded and peeling from the worn wood.

Jack smiled. "They did keep detailed records." His dark gaze studied her face. "And I've been through them all with a fine-tooth comb. No mention of a cup."

"It's not the entire cup. We found the stem up in New York. You'd likely have either the base or the drinking vessel, so it could have been described differently if someone wasn't sure what it was. Why don't we look together at the ledgers from the lifetime of the first person to own it, and see if anything crops up?"

"Oh, there's nothing of his. He didn't build this house. Never even visited the island as far as we know. He drowned in a wreck with all his possessions."

Vicki frowned. "Then who founded this island and carried on the family line?"

"His son. Swam ashore and took over the place. He was only fifteen at the time, but fought off anyone who came near with some muskets and shot he salvaged. Eventually he managed to rob and swindle enough people to rebuild the family fortune. I'm sure he was a sweet boy."

"I'll bet." She lifted a brow. Meanwhile her heart was sinking. "So if his father had the cup, it would have gone down in the shipwreck."

"Along with all his plundered booty and his latest child bride."

She sucked in a breath. Jack was playing with her.

He'd known the item she came here to search for was long gone before she'd even climbed into his car. Then again, he was an undersea treasure hunter. "Did it happen far from here?"

"Not far at all. The boy washed ashore here, clinging to a piece of spar. Can't be more than a few miles."

"So let's find it."

Again his rich, deep laugh filled the big kitchen. "Sure! We'll just throw out a fishing line and reel it in. People have been looking for that boat for years."

Her ten-thousand-dollar share of the reward started to shrink in her mind. "And why haven't they found it?"

He shrugged. "Who knows?"

"Come on. I know you must have looked for it."

"I did, early on. Truth is, these waters are filled with old wrecks, and I've always stumbled across something else to keep me busy. The combination of Spanish treasure fleets sailing regularly from Havana crossed with yearly hurricanes makes this area rich pickings for a treasure hunter."

"But you have better equipment now than you did then." Excitement started to prickle her skin. "I bet there was treasure on that ship when it went down."

"No doubt." Jack's eyes rested on hers, humor sparkling in their depths. "I never thought I'd hear you begging to go on a treasure hunt with me."

"I'm not begging!"

"Not yet, but if I don't say yes, you will be."

His arrogance made her want to slap him. "I'm simply asking."

"No." He turned and walked across the kitchen, then out through a door on the far side where he disappeared from view.

Vicki stood staring after him for a moment, her mouth gaping open like a fish. Then she strode after him. She spotted him in a long, stone corridor. "What do you mean, no?"

He turned. "I mean, no, I won't take you out hunting for part of some crazy old cup. Though I'm damn sure curious about why you want it so bad."

"What if the legend is true, and the Drummonds won't be happy again until the pieces of the cup are reunited?" She lifted a brow, trying to look nonchalant. It was a stretch.

Jack raised his own brow in response. "From what I can tell, none of us is really suffering right now."

"And none of you is happily married, either." Though his cousin Sinclair would be soon, largely thanks to her meddling.

"Maybe that's why we're happy." He shrugged and kept walking.

"Were your parents happily married?" She hurried to keep up.

"You know they weren't. My mom took my dad to the cleaners in the divorce. She even got this island."

His mom was a famous Nicaraguan model, now on her fourth or fifth husband. "See? Sinclair's parents weren't happy, either. It's his mom who's the driving force behind the search for the cup. She doesn't want her son to suffer like she did."

"How is old Sinclair? Still trimming his hedge funds into topiaries?"

"Sinclair is a very nice man, I'll have you know. And he's just fallen in love, too."

"There goes your theory about the family curse."

"Get this. He and his newly beloved were secretly

pining for each other for years—she's his housekeeper—
and it wasn't until they started looking for the cup that
they finally hooked up." She didn't mention her own
fairy godmother-esque role in shoving them together.

He reached a carved wooden door and rested one big
hand on the handle. "How sweet. What if I don't want
to fall in love?"

"Maybe you already have."

"With you?" His dark eyes twinkled.

"With yourself." How could he still look so handsome? You'd think all that sun and salt air would have
wizened him into a raisin. Instead he looked bronzed
and burnished like a fine statue from ancient Greece,
ready to throw a discus in the Olympics or besiege a
walled city. His body had filled out a little in the past
few years—all hard muscle, of course. Lucky thing
she wasn't as soft as she used to be or she'd be in danger of falling for him all over again. "Okay, that was
uncalled for. You're surprisingly modest, considering
your accomplishments. And I don't suppose you have
any shortage of women madly in love with you at any
given time."

"You're right, though." He looked thoughtful.

"You do love yourself?"

"No. That I've never fallen in love. Not really." His
eyes darkened and he looked as if he was about to say
something else but didn't.

She wanted to make a quip about how he'd been pining for her all those years, but she didn't speak, either.
Too much wishful thinking or something. "And you
think it's time you did?"

Still hovering outside the door, he rubbed at the muscle of his left arm. "I do want children."

Her eyes widened. Jack Drummond wanting a family? She didn't believe it. Maybe he was winding her up. "Maybe some will wash ashore in the next storm."

"You think I'm kidding, but I'm not. I like kids. They're fun. They bring a different perspective to everything, and they enjoy toys as much as I do."

Vicki laughed. "You're always full of surprises, Jack. So why don't you have any rugrats running around Castle Drummond?"

"Haven't met their mom yet." He held her gaze while he tilted his head. "At least I don't think I have." His voice contained the tiniest hint of suggestion. Was he playing with her? In that case he might be playing right into her hands.

"See? You need to find the cup so you can find Mrs. Right and start building your team. Let's look at some of those big complicated maps you love and see if we can figure out where the wreck is." She moved toward him. She could tell he was at least slightly interested, despite his protests.

"I see you know the way to a man's heart is through his nautical maps." He finally turned the handle and pushed open the door. "But first, let's go to bed."

Two

Jack walked into the bedroom, knowing Vicki would follow. She thought herself wild and unpredictable, but he knew better. She wanted that old cup for some reason and she was very determined in pursuit of a goal.

He couldn't resist turning to enjoy her expression. As expected, she'd walked coolly in behind him and was surveying the space. "Nice. Is that bed French?"

"Might be." The big oak monstrosity had been there since the house was built.

"I bet it could tell a few tales." She walked over to the headboard and examined the carved decoration.

"Lucky thing it's discreet." He swung himself onto the bed and relaxed, arms behind his head. "Come on in."

"You didn't seriously lure me in here in hope of seducing me, did you?"

"Hope springs eternal."

"I didn't know you were such a bright-eyed optimist."

"You have to be an optimist in the treasure hunting game. Eyes on the prize."

Vicki's almost-black hair was tied up in a messy bun, with tendrils falling about those adorable ears he still remembered nibbling. He let his eyes drift lower. She wore a black top that appeared to be made from pieces of ripped T-shirt, sewn back together. Knowing her it was probably from Paris and cost two thousand bucks. It hid her slender shape, but he knew that under its mysterious black layers was a lithe body with high, pointy breasts, and a stomach you could bounce gold doubloons off. A broad leather belt was slung across her hips, atop a pair of jeans that encased her long, slim legs. Desire crept through him, hot and relentless, like bootleg rum in his blood. "And the prize is tempting as ever."

"I see you haven't grown more subtle in your old age."

"Not much wiser, either. How about you?"

"I seem to get dumber every year." A smile tugged at her cheeky mouth. Vicki's lips were always dark, as if she wore lipstick, but he knew from kissing them that it was her hot blood close to the surface. "Otherwise, why would I be back here?"

"Because you couldn't get me out of your system." He narrowed his eyes and watched her reaction. Of course it was wishful thinking on his part. She'd probably forgotten him ten minutes after he left. He'd certainly hoped so at the time. Things had gotten way too intense and it was time to lift anchor and run for the open sea.

"You've been out of my system almost as long as the last dregs of nicotine from another one of my bad habits." She lifted her chin. "So don't get any ideas that I'm here for you. I'm just here because I *need* you."

"Be still, my heart." He placed a hand over it and wasn't surprised to find it beating faster than usual. Vicki must have that effect on any man. "Come lie next to me."

"No way."

"It's important."

"Nothing's that important." She'd crossed her arms in a defensive posture, and her hips tilted at a defiant angle. Sense memory flashed a moment of luscious recall—her hips pressed against his, arching higher, driving them both to a realm of beauty and madness.

"Not even finding your precious cup?"

"I fail to see how climbing into the sack with you brings me closer to my goal."

He raised a brow. "I always thought you were a lateral thinker. The thing is, you need to join me in bed to see how things lie."

She pursed her lips slightly and shifted her weight onto her other foot. Her pale violet eyes viewed him with intense suspicion. "I can see how things lie from right here."

"No, you can't." He glanced up at the ceiling. Time had faded and darkened the image. The plaster had cracked in places, but the fresco still showed the green shore of the island against the pale blue of the sea. "Come on. Hop up." He tapped the sheets. "So you can take a look at the old family map."

"What?" She peered upward, but he knew she couldn't see anything. The edge of the four-poster bed blocked any view of the painting unless one was literally lying on the mattress.

"Lazaro Drummond—the shipwreck survivor—painted the map above his bed, so that no one could see it but him."

"And his lovers."

He let a slow smile creep across his mouth. "Exactly."

Vicki walked toward the bed and climbed gingerly onto the opposite side. She settled herself on her back with her head on the pillow. He studied her for signs that she was uncomfortable—or excited—by being next to him on a bed. But no, she was entirely riveted by the painting overhead. She stared at it without speaking, almost without breathing, for a full minute. "I do believe this is the first real-life treasure map I've ever seen."

"They never do look like the ones in the movies." He enjoyed the fascinated expression on her face. How long had it been since he kissed that sassy mouth? Six years, at least. The urge to repeat history was rising in his blood.

"I keep looking for the X but I can't see it."

"The mermaid sitting on the rock. She's the X."

"Hmm." Vicki stared at it thoughtfully. She hadn't moved her eyes from the ceiling since the moment she lay down. "So the wreck is southeast of the island. Is there any kind of distance scale so we know how far it is?"

"If the size of the island is accurately drawn, it would be about two and a quarter miles off the northernmost inlet. That's what we Drummonds have always assumed anyway."

"And none of you has ever found it."

"Not yet." He shot her a sly glance.

She finally turned to look at him. Her pale eyes sparkled like diamonds. "That's why I'm here."

"I can believe you bring luck."

"Luck? How about my sharp mind?" She looked back up at the painting.

He felt as if the sun had shifted and thrown him into shadow. He wanted that bright, hopeful gaze on him again. "What will you do for me if I find it for you?" He made sure his voice held a purr of suggestion.

"Do for you? You'll get all the loot your ancestor stole and took to the bottom of the ocean with him. Isn't that enough?"

"There's never enough." He stared at her, willing her to bless him with her radiance again.

She turned to him, cheek resting on the soft pillow. "What else did you have in mind?" Dark lashes framed her eyes, giving them a smoky, sultry look. Her soft, pink mouth looked ripe with promise. He could easily imagine leaning forward a few inches and pressing his lips to hers.

Arousal thickened his groin and made his breath come faster. "I like having you back in my bed again." Her mouth twitched slightly, which was almost unbearably sensual. "If you'll stay with me here in my bed while we search, I'll plumb the depths of the ocean for you."

Her eyes widened. "That's a big ask."

"So's yours. I've got projects lined up that could keep me busy until 2050. You're asking me to drop everything and go fishing around on the bottom of the ocean for a wreck people have been hunting for more than 250 years. It won't be easy to find, that's for sure."

"You don't like things too easy, though, do you, Jack?"

He laughed. "No, Vicki, I don't."

"Then I can hardly just agree to your command, can I?" She sprang off the bed and strode from the room before he could even gather his thoughts, which were scattered and distracted by the sight of her tight ass in those fitted jeans.

She knew him too well.

"So where's the boat?" Vicki headed into the big living room, past the dark pieces of ancient furniture. Lucky thing she could still remember her way around somewhat. She tried a handle on one of the French doors, which opened out onto a broad, stone terrace.

"At the dock."

"Not the one we came on. Your super-high-tech treasure hunting boat."

"Ah. That's hidden."

"More valuable than the treasure it finds?"

"Something like that." Jack followed her out onto the terrace and squinted in the afternoon sun.

Damn but she'd been tempted to take him up on his offer. He had looked almost irresistible, lying there relaxed, heavy and sexy as hell, muscles sinking into the soft mattress, and that cool, curious look on his face.

But as she'd observed, he didn't like things too easy. He got bored quickly. Anyone wanting to keep Jack's interest better keep him guessing. And she'd already failed at that once, so the pressure was on.

"You trust me, don't you?" She smiled sweetly at him.

That lazy, puma grin sneaked back across his mouth. "At least as far as I can throw you." He took a step forward and her muscles tightened as she read sudden intention in his body. "Let's see exactly how far that is."

His arms reached out and she shrieked and ran—down the wide steps and onto a scraggly lawn. She ducked left and looked for an opening in the sea grape hedge, but it was too late. Jack's hands caught her around the waist and clutched her against him.

Breath flew from her lungs, less from force and more from the emotional impact of feeling Jack's big arms around her again. She braced herself, waiting for him to pick her up and hurl her somewhere. Instead, his grip only tightened and she felt his warm breath on the back of her neck.

Desire unfurled inside her, hot and liquid, darting through her veins and loosening her from head to toe. She could turn around right now and kiss him full on the mouth—but that would end the chase, and the chase excited him. "You wouldn't take advantage of a defenseless maiden, would you?"

"No way. But you? Sure." She could feel his grin radiating into the back of her brain. Still, his hands didn't stray from her waist. She found herself wanting them to.

"So you're not going to throw me?"

"Apparently I can't."

"Too soft?"

"Something like that. But it doesn't say much for how far I can trust you." He leaned in closer and his hot breath tickled her neck. "Though, strangely, I do trust you. You've never deceived me or led me astray." He sounded thoughtful. "At least not that I'm aware of."

"And I don't plan to start now." She wanted to move. Being so close to Jack, with his arms around her and her back pressed to his hard chest, was starting to mess with her mind. Worse yet, her body was starting to act up. Nipples thickening against her shirt, belly quivering, knees growing unreliable. If he hadn't already noticed, he might soon, and she'd rather die than have him know that he still had power over her.

"So, your precious ship. In some hidden cove, I'm guessing?"

"Nope, it's at the deeper dock." His hands pulled way from her waist slowly. Relief mingled with a surprise ripple of sadness. "Follow me." He pulled right away from her and set off across the lawn. Abandoned by his warm attentions, her skin felt cold. Still, she had to keep the dance going. It wouldn't work if he had his fill of her before they even got started. She was in control this time and she intended to keep it that way.

Jack's treasure hunting boat was dark blue, faded by the sun. It didn't look especially precious or expensive, but then probably the treasure it found didn't, either—at first.

Jack climbed aboard, muscles flexing beneath his faded jeans. "Done much diving lately?"

"Nope."

"Can you still remember how?"

"More or less." Jack had shown her how to dive years ago. Breathing underwater felt horribly unnatural and she'd been a slow study. She'd only fought past her fears out of sheer determination to prove he was wrong when he'd said she'd never do it. She wasn't too excited about doing it again. "Do we need to dive? Don't you have sonar to find the ship and a team of nano-robots to crawl the ocean floor for artifacts these days?"

He laughed. "That would take all the fun out of it." He reached down a hand and, with some misgivings, she grasped it and let him help as she climbed onto the shifting deck. "We sometimes use sonar to look for a wreck, though it doesn't always help. These funnels are used to blow holes in the ocean floor to expose stuff that's buried under the sand. After that, it's all about having sharp eyes and a lot of patience."

"You don't strike me as the patient type." She squinted in the sun. The boat was neat as a pin, every rope coiled to perfection and the surfaces scrubbed to eye-popping white.

"I'm as patient as they come." His slow, lazy smile challenged her to disagree. "I'll wait a whole lifetime for something if it's worth waiting for."

"Intriguing." She peered at the controls of the boat. It was probably not that much harder to maneuver than a car, should the need arise. "I suppose that's why you've never married."

"Who says I've never married?" His reply made her head snap up, which she bitterly regretted when she saw his smile broaden. "I only said that I've never fallen in love. But I'm touched that you care."

"So, have you?" She tried to look casual, walking to another part of the deck. The idea of Jack pledging himself to another woman for an entire lifetime made her stomach tighten. Which was ridiculous. Why would she care?

"Not yet."

Relief sank through her. Probably because she didn't need any more complications right now, like some damsel coming forward to claim that the treasure was half hers as a result of their divorce settlement.

"But I might have."

"If there was someone out there crazy enough to take you."

"I like crazy broads." His lazy gaze grazed her body, setting her skin on fire through her clothes and igniting a flash of irritation inside her.

"Why doesn't that surprise me?"

"Probably why I liked *you* so much." He hadn't taken his eyes off her, and his dark stare seemed to penetrate right through her. Why did she still have to be so attracted to him? You'd think that kind of thing would fade over time. She thought it had! But now that she was right here, only a few sun-scorched feet from him, all that long-forgotten desire was rising up like buried treasure—or junk—hidden beneath shifting sands.

"I don't think you liked me all that much." She walked to the prow of the boat, careful to keep her footing on the slippery surface. The deck rose and fell with the constant heave of the ocean, and she had to work slightly to stay balanced. "But maybe I'm wrong." She turned to him, feeling safer with slightly more distance between them.

"Maybe you are." His forehead was slightly furrowed, and his eyes rested on her for such a long time that she almost lost her footing and had to grab the rail around the deck. Was he thinking back to their whirlwind romance, all those sweltering nights in the Keys that one summer after college? She didn't think about it much, not anymore. She was over it.

Truth be told, though, she wasn't entirely over getting dumped at the end of their steamy romance. And if the spark between them should happen to get reignited, she looked forward to returning the favor.

The rise and fall of the ocean shifted the deck under her feet and her stomach was starting to feel queasy. If Jack knew, he'd make fun of her for not having her sea legs. "So, shall we plan to start the search tomorrow?" Then she'd have time to take a seasickness remedy in advance.

"I don't know." He stared out at the horizon, squinting out at the deep, blue unknown, sun blazing on his hard features. He was taunting her. He turned to look at her and her stomach lurched. "Did you think about my proposal?"

"I suppose it does make sense to spend time under the map together. To study it." Anywhere other than here on this lurching deck. She grabbed a handrail, trying to look casual. It was surprising how little movement it took to throw your inner ear off kilter. And what an unhappy effect that had on the stomach.

"It'll be like old times." His voice held more than a hint of suggestion.

Without waiting for an invitation, she clambered over the side of the boat—with some difficulty, which she attempted to conceal—and back onto the hard and very still dock. "Not really." This time she'd be in control of what happened, and when it ended.

"Leaving so soon? I was going to show you the sonar."

"I'll see it in action tomorrow." She marched up the dock toward the house, hoping she could make it back there and collapse somewhere fast. She didn't intend for Jack to see her in a moment of weakness. Like the predator he was, he'd have to pounce and play with her, and she wasn't quite strong enough for that.

Once she had the reward, though, she'd feel strong. Ten thousand dollars might not sound like much to her old friends, but it would be enough to sow the seeds of her new life. A life where she wouldn't have to depend on anybody but herself.

She heard the thud of Jack's feet hitting the deck. He was coming after her. A satisfied smile crossed her mouth. She made sure to add an extra ounce of swagger to her walk, knowing—or was it hoping?—that his eyes were tracking her hips like a laser beam.

He thought he'd achieved a victory by getting her to agree to sleep with him. Little did he know it had been her plan all along. She'd enjoy it, too. She hadn't chanced a sensual affair in almost a year. She'd been too busy dodging creditors and trying to hide her precarious financial situation. She certainly hadn't wanted to be in an intimate situation where she might have to open up to someone.

She wouldn't have to open up to Jack. His personal walls were as thick as the battlements on his ancestral home, and he never let them down. They could make love all night long and keep their hearts under lock and key. Hers had chains on it that weren't likely to break anytime soon, especially not for Jack Drummond.

His footsteps were gaining on her, and she fought the urge to walk faster. Instead, she slowed to let him catch up. "Is there any hope of dinner out here on your desert island?"

"I caught a big swordfish yesterday. We can grill it."

"I thought we weren't supposed to eat swordfish any-more now that we've poisoned the oceans. A friend of mine is pregnant and she said the doctor told her the toxins can affect your genes and damage your future children."

"My children might enjoy having three eyes." His grin cut a white slash across his dark face. "Are you worried about your own offspring?"

"I won't ever have children." She said it brightly. "So I can eat all the swordfish I want."

His smile vanished. "You can't have kids?"

She startled at the sudden change in his demeanor. Why did he care if she could have children or not? "Not can't, *won't*. I'm not cut out for motherhood. Too much wiping butts and drying tears for my taste."

He laughed. "Did your mom do those things?"

"No, she hired a nanny for that." She walked faster. This conversation was getting too personal.

"You could do the same." She felt his dark, penetrating gaze on her cheek.

"No, thanks. I'm doing my best not to turn out like my parents."

"Me, too. Unlike my dad, I intend to be alive at fifty." Something in his voice made her turn to look at him. His eyes were shadowed.

"I heard about his death. I'm sorry. It was a small-plane accident, wasn't it?"

"It was no accident." He marched steadily, eyes now straight ahead. The house loomed through the trees. "He'd been trying to kill himself for years."

The Drummond curse. Vicki remembered Katherine Drummond begging her to help her find the lost cup pieces and lift the curse that had dogged the family for centuries. At first Vicki had laughed it off, but the Drummonds certainly didn't seem to have much luck in life. They could make money all day long, but when it came to marriage or family harmony, or even simple contentment, they were a disaster zone.

"The awkward silence descends." Jack spoke softly, slightly mocking. "So, the swordfish it is. Let our children learn to play with the dark hand they're dealt."

"I'm sure it will be delicious." She regretted her quip about the fish. "I eat it all the time and love it."

"I remember it being your favorite." He opened a side door of the house, pushing at the big, tarnished brass handle. Something in the tone of his voice made her breath catch at the bottom of her lungs. What else did he remember? How she'd called him in the middle of the night just to hear the sound of his voice? The way she sighed when he kissed her neck?

The time she'd made the bitter mistake of telling him she loved him.

That last one wasn't a question. He probably would remember that, unless he'd repressed it somehow. That little slip of the tongue had sent him running.

She followed him into the cool, shaded interior. Things would be a lot easier if she could find this cup without his help. Just her luck, it had wound up on the bottom of the sea. Even if they could find the ship, it would be a miracle if the cup piece hadn't washed away, and then again, if it were recognizable enough for her to find it. This could well be a wild goose chase, and she couldn't afford to waste too much time on it. She should probably set a strict deadline for herself, with plans to jump ship if they hadn't found it within two weeks.

"You're quieter than you used to be." His words startled her from her thoughts.

"More going on in my brain, less coming out of

my mouth." She smiled and leaned against the kitchen counter.

"How enigmatic." He pulled a bottle of wine from a large rack against one wall. "Pinot grigio?"

"Sure." She watched his hands as he peeled away the foil over the cork. His fingers were precise and careful, no doubt good with fine detail and careful with precious relics. He plunged the corkscrew in with gusto—the kind of thrust with which he approached most aspects of life—and turned it aggressively. The muscles in his forearms torqued beneath the skin, revealing their power and stirring something primal inside her.

It had to be primal because it had nothing to do with modern-day common sense. Men didn't need strength to be successful in today's world. A good head for numbers and a dubious set of morals was a much more effective get-rich-quick kit.

Still, she admired the bulge of his biceps against the soft sleeve of his T-shirt as he pulled the cork from the bottle in a swift and brutal movement. The cork squeaked and popped free, leaving her heart beating slightly faster.

She distracted herself by admiring the interesting tile work on the wall behind the stove. No sense getting herself too aroused and invested in their evening plans. She might need to pull back at some point and she didn't want her own rampant desires to make that almost impossible.

Jack handed her a brimming glass of pale gold wine. "To treasure."

"Treasure." She smiled and lifted her glass. The wine tasted delicious, smooth, rich, cool and refreshing after the hot sun outside. "Jewels and coins and gold bars for you, part of an old cup for me."

"That doesn't sound fair." His dark eyes sparkled behind the lock of hair hanging down to them. "Maybe we'll have to find you a gold necklace or a stash of rings."

She held out one of her pale, bony hands. "As you can see, I'm not much of a ring wearer."

"You might change your mind, for the right one."

"Don't count on it." She glanced at her empty ring finger. She did not intend to live her life by anyone else's rules. "But I'd be happy to sell it for a handsome profit." She shone him a bright smile. "In fact, that's my intended future business, so it would be a nice jump start."

"I heard you were working for an auction house."

"That was my apprenticeship. Now that I know what things are worth, I plan to go out on my own." She sipped her wine again. "This is good stuff. Tastes expensive."

"You do know what things are worth." His eyes crinkled in a smile.

"You're funny, Jack. You always look so casual and act like you don't care about money, but you do enjoy the finer things in life."

"One of my many weaknesses."

"Hmm, makes me wonder what your other weaknesses are." Not a soft heart, for sure. Which is why he'd never fallen for anyone.

"A passion for a fickle mistress." He looked at her over his glass.

"The sea." She knew it wouldn't be a real woman.

He nodded. "Though she's been good to me."

"She's giving you all the riches she took from the

hundreds of men and women who've died off this coast over the centuries."

"I did say she was fickle."

"And obviously has her favorites."

A slow smile crept across his mouth. "Let's go sit where we can see her." He led the way out onto a veranda with a view out over the sea grape in the dunes. Blue and steady, the ocean lay before them like a velvet throw. She could hear the waves crashing on the beach, but couldn't see them because they were hidden by the dunes. Jack ushered her to sit on a sleek upholstered outdoor sofa. When she was seated, he eased himself down next to her and flung his arm casually on the back of the sofa behind her.

Her neck and shoulders prickled with awareness. Of course he was doing it deliberately. He wanted to taunt and tempt her. He had every intention of seducing her. And she might even let him, but not until they were at least on the way to finding the cup. Otherwise he might find he'd already got what he wanted and send her packing.

She twisted the stem of her wineglass in her hands. "Because there's a reward, there are probably other people looking. We need to move fast."

"We'll start tomorrow at first light."

"When is that?"

"Six or so is when you can start to tell the sea from the shore."

She cringed inwardly. Jack probably didn't even drink coffee in the morning. She usually started the day with her familiar newspapers and a hearty meal to ground herself before venturing out into the cold, cruel world. The prospect of having to drag herself out of bed and onto the sea without those reassuring comforts was frightening. And she'd better buy something for her stomach. If she'd known the cup was under the sea, she might have been better prepared. "Where's the nearest drugstore?"

"Headache?"

She hesitated. "Nope. I might need a little something for my stomach on the boat tomorrow." She avoided his eyes. "It's always good to be prepared."

"Don't worry. My larder's well stocked." His eyes twinkled. Maybe he'd give her a placebo so she'd be leaning over the edge of the deck, begging for mercy. "We can stay out at sea for days at a time. Weeks even."

"I'm not sure I'd survive weeks trapped on a boat with you, Jack."

"I suspect you could survive almost anything." His arm shifted behind her, and she tried to ignore the shimmer of response that slid through her body. "You look slender and insubstantial on the outside, but you're made of sturdy stuff."

"I hope so." She'd need to be to make it through this trial. Being this close to Jack was having a dangerous effect on her sanity. Which didn't make any sense. He was just another rich, handsome bozo and she had years of experience and training in dealing with them. "I guess only time will tell."

"You look different." His eyes narrowed. He studied her face for a moment while her pulse quickened.

"It has been six years since I saw you." Did she look older? Her dad had aged dramatically during his swift and private fall from grace. Hollows appeared under his eyes and cheekbones, and his skin developed a bluish undertone. "You, on the other hand, look exactly the same."

Not exactly. Time and the sun, working hand in hand, had made him look rugged and distinguished. His eyes still had that insolent flash to them, and his lip that disdainful way of curving upward so you couldn't tell if he was laughing with you or at you.

Did she imagine it or did his left thigh creep imperceptibly closer to her right one? She could almost feel the heat of it through her pants. The salt air filled her lungs and made her giddy.

"I don't know what exactly is different." His eyes rested on her face—her cheek, to be precise, because she was avoiding his gaze by staring at the horizon. "Something big, though."

She shrank a little under his inquisitive look. She was quite a different person than the brash, confident and empty-headed girl who'd partied and had sex on the beach with him that summer. Then she'd thought the world was hers for the taking and she was taking a vacation before seizing it. The years since had taught her that the world wasn't too interested in whether she wanted it and that the foundation of her life—the privilege and wealth afforded by her proud family—had been built on the shifting sands of illusion.

She certainly didn't intend for him to find out about that. No, they could laugh about that later once she'd made a name for herself and didn't need to rest on anyone else's laurels. Right now, though, she was hanging in thin air, and she intended to keep that a secret.

Which might be interesting, because she'd already committed to sharing a bed with him. Hopefully she wouldn't talk in her sleep.

Three

Jack grilled his delicious swordfish and served it with skewered grilled vegetables out on the terrace, where the evening breeze kept bugs at bay. They could see the lights of fishing boats and the occasional cruise ship in the distance, but all was stillness and silence on the island.

"It's so peaceful here." Vicki looked out over the dunes. "Doesn't it drive you nuts?"

"Maybe that's why I've always been nuts." Jack reclined in his chair. Lit tapers in the gnarled old candelabra on the table cast flickering shadows over his hard features. "I need it, though. Helps me recharge my batteries."

"Hmm. I can just hook myself up to my car engine by the jumper cables." She sipped her wine, then, realizing she'd had almost three glasses, pushed her wineglass out of reach. She was in danger of becoming tipsy. She'd better work on keeping her hatches more tightly battened.

"You still like living in the city?" Jack lifted his arms and placed them behind his head, giving her a breath-stealing view of his powerful biceps.

She swallowed and squinted slightly to obscure the view. "Yes. I think I love being another anonymous face in the crowd. I can't imagine living in a small town where everyone knows who I am."

"Sounds like you're running from something. Or someone."

"Maybe I prefer being out of reach." She smiled and made a conscious effort not to pick up her glass again. If only they could go to bed so she could stop trying to put on a bravely charming front. Then again, that might be leaping from the frying pan into the fire.

"Did you ever think about me, you know, over the years?" His voice was low, gruff.

"Certainly not. You dumped me, remember?" Her adrenaline level jumped. This had to come out sooner or later. Might as well get it over with.

"I always felt bad about the way I took off. Blame it on youthful immaturity."

She sneaked a glance at him. It was hard to read his expression in the flickering candlelight, but she imagined she saw a hint of sheepishness in his eyes. "Don't flatter yourself that I've spent the last few years pining over you. I've had far more traumatic relationships since." She inhaled the sea air.

"Have you? Did someone break your heart?"

"No way. Nothing in there but cogs and wheels. That's why I can jump-start my battery so easily." A sudden chill in the night air made goose bumps spring up on her arms, and she rubbed them. "Things may be a little rusty, but nothing's broken."

He chuckled. "I've got some oil for your rusty gears."

"I bet you do." She looked at him down the length of her nose. She had to work hard not to smile. It was almost impossible to be mad at Jack Drummond when she was in his presence. That came later, when she realized how he'd played her like a violin. "But you can leave it on your garage shelf. I like to think of my rust as a protective barrier."

"I'm feeling jealous." His annoyingly thick biceps flexed as he stretched. "I'm beginning to think I made a big mistake back then."

"One of many, I'd imagine." Again, she had to fight the reflex to reach for her wine. Shame she didn't smoke. It was hard not to fidget, but she worked hard to look cool and calm.

"You know it." That familiar lazy grin eased across his mouth. "But they've been fun, each and every one."

"Just think of all the fun we'd have missed out on if we'd fallen madly in love with each other and done something stupid like getting married." She hugged herself. It was getting colder. "That would have been quite the act of rebellion at the time."

He laughed. "Yes, your parents might have died of shock at the prospect of their princess marrying a beach bum."

"Until they realized how filthy rich you are. Then they'd have staged a brisk recovery and welcomed you with open arms. It would have all been very boring."

"I spared us that by running off like a coward at the first sign of emotion."

She froze. He'd just admitted it. That he remembered. *I love you.*

She'd said it loud and clear, for the one and only time in her life. She'd rather slit her own throat than ever utter those three words again. "Emotion? I'm not sure I was ever capable of one of those."

"Me, either. Inconvenient and messy things. Best left to those who don't have enough going on in their lives. Speaking of which, we should get to bed." His eyes flashed, creating a frightening jolt of response somewhere low in her belly. "Because we need to get up early in the morning, of course." His steady, dark gaze suggested more than sleep.

Suddenly her plan to enjoy the pleasures of his body seemed like the dumbest idea she'd ever come up with. Maybe because she was tired and all this talk of old hurts made her feel vulnerable. "Do you sleep in that same room, under the map?"

"Of course. It's always been the captain's bedroom." He grabbed the bottle and glasses from the table. She hesitated for a second before taking their plates and cutlery. She'd become used to being waited on hand and foot in Sinclair Drummond's house—by the woman he'd recently become engaged to.

"That map must be emblazoned on your brain by now."

"Hasn't helped me find the treasure, though."

"Maybe you're reading it wrong?" They walked back into the air-conditioned calm of the house. "Perhaps what it needs is a different perspective." She didn't want to speculate on how many women's eyes had stared up at that map over the centuries.

"I'll welcome your angle on it. I think we've read it every possible way it can be read."

"But you've never found the ship."

"The ship could be broken up and washed away by now."

And the cup gone forever. "It's out there. I feel it in my bones." She shot him a glance as they walked side by side down the hallway to the bedroom.

"I would definitely bet money on your intuition."

"You should. I hooked your cousin Sinclair up with his new bride. The moment I saw the way they looked at each other, I knew they were meant to be together."

"Were they dating?"

"Nope, she was serving him his morning coffee and ironing his linen napkins, but I made sure Cinderella went to the ball with her handsome prince and it's been all uphill from there." Well, mostly. No need to mention the part about his horrid ex-wife suddenly discovering she was pregnant. "He certainly believes in my hunches now."

"Then I'll bet on them, too, and put my equipment and expertise at your disposal."

He opened the door to the bedroom, dimly lit by wall sconces that cast a romantic glow over the old plasterwork. The bed looked much smaller than she remembered, its massive wood structure framing what was probably only a full-size mattress. "It's going to be a tight fit for both of us."

"All the better." His feral grin flashed for a brief second. Then a more gentlemanly expression returned. "I'll leave you to get changed while I lock up for the night."

"Lock up? We're on an island. Who are you trying to keep out?"

"Maybe you should ask who I'm trying to keep in."

He vanished before she could come up with a witty reply. Or any reply. Her suitcase stood silently in one corner, and she hurried to get changed into her pj's before he could come back and watch her undress.

She donned a bra and panties as extra armor underneath her white cotton camisole and lounge pants. Not that she expected him to do anything mischievous while she was asleep. That wasn't his style. There was absolutely nothing sneaky about Jack Drummond. If he planned to lay siege, he'd do it while she was wide-awake.

It was her own defenses she was worried about. She didn't want any part of her to start straying toward his side of the mattress, hoping for a casual brush against those thick biceps or one of those powerful thighs. Much better to keep everything strapped down and swathed in fabric.

She washed her face in the big onyx sink. The mirror was ancient, foggy and flecked with dark spots. When she caught sight of her reflection, it startled her. It was as if she'd seen a dream version of herself, pale and wan, lost in a strange world. She turned away sharply. When she walked back into the bedroom, Jack was there, casually stripping away his clothes and revealing his tanned physique. She made a valiant effort not to look, but it was hard because he faced the opposite direction and she had free rein to indulge an academic interest in seeing how his body compared to the one in her memory.

Favorably. She had to admire the way he'd filled out. Not a rangy, sunburned youth anymore, but a man in his prime. Broad-shouldered enough to carry the weight of the world. When his jeans slid down, she gasped at how pale his backside was. Obviously the only part of him that never got much sun exposure.

He must have heard her intake of breath because he turned his head. "I hope I'm not being rude by stripping off right here. You have seen it all before."

"It's your bedroom. You do what you like." She grabbed her phone from her purse, so she could distract herself by checking her messages, then walked to the bed and climbed in, with some difficulty because it was high. She slid under the covers and was gratified to find soft sheets there. Once again, only the best for Jack Drummond. She turned on her phone and checked her texts. Nothing interesting. Her gaze drifted up to the mural painted overhead. The green shoreline, dotted with palm trees, the blue sea, the crudely painted mermaid sitting on her rock. No one would call it a work of art. The fresco obviously hadn't ever been restored, either. Even the scant light from her phone picked out the uneven surface and revealed where tiny chips of plaster had flaked off. It was darkened by centuries of smoke from candles and pipes and who knew what else Jack's pirate ancestors had burned in here. It would be interesting to see what a good cleaning might reveal.

"How did you measure the distances on the map to know where to look?" She kept her eyes firmly off Jack as he walked toward the bed—still naked, as far as she could tell—and climbed under the covers.

"We started a few yards off the shore and kept moving out north at the same angle. It wasn't too scientific. In all honesty I put nearly two years into it and I'm sure I wasn't the first."

"One of your ancestors could have found the wreck and salvaged it." Her skin tingled with uncomfortable awareness that his naked body shared the same dark, small space with hers.

"Found it maybe. Salvaged it? Impossible. There's a steep shelf offshore and the wreck is somewhere outside the shelf. The water's way too deep for anyone without sophisticated equipment like oxygen tanks to explore. No way it could have been done before the twentieth century, and if it was that recent I'd know about it."

He rolled toward her, so close she could almost feel his hot breath on her skin. Her nerve endings pulsed and tingled—with the desire to leap out of this bed and save herself. She managed, with great effort, to keep her eyes on the low ceiling above the bed. What she saw there made her squint her eyes in an effort to focus more closely. In the dim half light from her phone the shadowy pits in the plaster stirred adrenaline in her blood. "Do you have a flashlight?"

"Sure." She heard him turn and reach behind him. "Keep one next to the bed at all times. We often lose power during storms."

She turned to take it and got a disarming eyeful of his tanned pecs. "Thanks." She climbed out from under the covers, careful not to accidentally dislodge them from any more of his bare flesh, and stood on the mattress. Holding the flashlight above her head, she shone it at the ceiling. "Interesting." Her pulse quickened and she moved her arm higher, trying to keep her balance on the squishy surface of the mattress, which was already thrown off balance by Jack's heavy form.

"What do you see?"

"The plaster has some tiny chips, but there's still color behind them. I think there's another painting underneath this one."

"You're kidding." She braced as he shifted the mattress by sitting up.

"You should already know I'm not the jolly jokester type." Gingerly she reached up and touched one of the indentations in the surface. She scraped the edge of the hole lightly with her fingernail—museum curators would shudder—and tiny fragments of plaster came away, but the surface beneath stayed intact. And was definitely pigmented. "I wonder if one of your sneaky ancestors covered up the real map with a misleading one to put someone else off the scent."

"If they did, it's worked very well. How do you remove the top layer?"

"It looks like someone slathered a fresh layer of plaster over a previous painting. If that's the case we should be able to chip it off. Look…" She pointed to the chip in the fresco. "There's a patch of blue underneath this green area. That's what makes me think there's another picture."

Jack rose to his feet, shifting the entire mattress in his direction. She struggled to keep her footing, but had to put out a hand and steady herself on the rock-hard muscle of his torso. Once she had her balance again, she snatched her hand back as if his skin had burned it. "Of course, chipping it off will destroy the painting. I know it's part of your family history."

"We Drummonds have far too much family history."

"There are ways of lifting it off, using glue and fabric to transfer it to a new surface, but we'd have to hunt down the materials and I've never done it before, so it would take some research and experimentation…."

"I'll go get a couple of chisels." Jack jumped off the bed, throwing her off balance again. She had to steady herself by thrusting her arm up toward the ceiling. Where her fingers met the surface she could swear she felt it crack slightly, ready to release it's grip on the ceiling above and fall away to reveal its secrets.

Jack had left the room, so she took a moment to heave a tiny sigh of relief. Instead of an awkward night beneath the sheets with him, it looked as though they were in for an interesting night of discovery.

Either that or she was about to destroy a Drummond family heirloom. She pulled her camera from her bag and took about fifty pictures of the painting from all angles, in case removing it should prove to be a mistake.

Jack returned a minute later with an armory of tools in a wooden box, and some khaki shorts—thank goodness—covering his man bits. She rifled through the box and chose an ancient flat-head screwdriver and a tiny hammer. "We want to use something blunt, so we don't chip right through it. Hopefully if we can crack the surface it will fall away like it's already started to do."

She started first, chipping gently next to one of the existing holes. Spider cracks crawled slowly across the plaster, a few millimeters at a time. She was barely breathing. This could all be a stupid mistake—someone might have just painted the wall a flat color before creating the map. She kept going, though, and after about two minutes, a tiny chunk of plaster no larger than a pinky nail fell to the sheets below. Underneath it was more of the rich indigo-blue color she'd glimpsed. "You'd better get a drop cloth for the bed or your sheets will get dusty." She spoke through a smile.

"Never mind that." Jack picked up the little hammer and began tapping. "I can't believe I've slept under this thing for years and never thought to look beneath the surface."

"Then it's rather a miracle that I came back into your life, isn't it?"

"Indeed it is."

Jack's arm ached from holding it over his head while tapping at the fresco. They couldn't risk being too aggressive and damaging the painting beneath, so it was slow going. As 3:00 a.m. rolled past, they'd revealed enough to see that there was indeed another map painted below in far richer and more saturated colors. This map showed only the shore of the island, a detailed outline with nooks and crannies and rock outcroppings. The rest of the painting, so far, was all indigo-blue sea. No sign of an *X*, or even a helpful mermaid.

"What do you think of all these white lines?" The blue ocean surface was crisscrossed with faint white hatch marks, which gave the appearance of ocean peaks and waves.

"Could be something to do with where the treasure is hidden. Or not." Vicki tapped away relentlessly at the plaster, which rained down on the bed, and sometimes on him, in a fine powder dust. "We'll know more once we can see the whole thing."

"How about a break?" His legs also ached from standing on the bed. It made the deck of a ship seem downright steady. But the sight of Vicki's lithe body, scant inches from his, kept his strength up enough to keep going.

"No way. We need to get out there tomorrow. There's a reward for the cup, remember?"

"How is anyone else supposed to find the cup when they don't even know it's under the sea?"

"They'll figure it out." She hadn't even glanced at him. Too wrapped up in her task. "Believe me, it won't be that hard. Something tells me there are books written about your ancestors and their treasure."

Jack shrugged. "I suppose. Still, the reward isn't large enough to draw the big treasure hunters."

"No, but the treasure is, and once other people start looking for it, they'll want in on the action. How would you feel if some metal detector hobbyist found it and claimed everything?"

"That might make me cry." He sneaked a sideways glance at her, and was rewarded by her turning to him. "But at least you'd be here to dry my tears."

"Don't count on it. I'll be out there cozying up to the finder." Her teeth flashed in a sudden smile that made his breath stick in his lungs. How could she still be so beautiful? The passing years had chiseled her girlish features to a fine perfection—high cheekbones and determined chin. Her eyes had a dimension he didn't remember seeing there, something wary and challenging that added depth to her proud beauty.

"So you'd ditch me for the winner."

"Wouldn't you do the same?"

"Probably." A grin pulled at his mouth. His arms, tired of all the chiseling, had fallen to his sides. "It's not easy talking to someone who knows me so well."

"Even after all these years, huh? I guess you haven't changed that much."

"I don't think I've changed at all." He put serious effort into not growing staid and boring like his former surfing buddies, with their McMansions and monster

SUVs. "And if you haven't changed, either, we're still a team to be reckoned with."

"Which is why we're not quitting on this fresco." Her arms were still raised and her tool tap-tap-tapping gently against the brittle plaster. Jack's eyes burned from the dust, but he was damned if he'd quit before she did. She wouldn't respect him, for one thing, and for some strange reason he didn't feel like analyzing, her respect was important to him. Suppressing a groan, he got back to the task, chipping away at his family history, when he'd much rather be stripping away Vicki's dusty pajamas and tasting the lush body hidden beneath them.

There'd be time for that later.

"I think this is some kind of code." Vicki murmured the words so low he could barely make them out. She'd stopped chiseling and was staring hard at the surface. "The white hatch marks. I keep seeing Roman numerals in them."

Jack stared at the pattern, which danced before his tired eyes. "Why would someone put hidden numbers on a map?"

"I don't know." She pressed a long, slender finger to the surface of the mural, smearing away the layer of dust left behind. The action pulled her T-shirt firmly across her delicious, pointy breasts, and he suddenly had to grab a bedpost to keep his balance. "Don't fall and hurt yourself."

The slight lift of her brow made him smile. Then he tried to focus on the painting again. He could make out vertical and horizontal lines that, when looked at with a forgiving eye, did look a bit like numbers. "I see what you mean." He reached up, partly to steady himself on the ceiling, truth be told, and partly to focus his tired vision on the spot he was trying to read. He made out a VIII. "This looks like an eight."

"And look, this is an *X,* it's just divided into two *V*s so it isn't so obvious."

"*X* marks the spot?" He squinted at the spot near her fingers.

"No way. That would be too easy. And look, there are loads of them."

"Great. I've always loved looking for needles in haystacks."

"Me, too." Her eyes were riveted on the painted surface. "There's a pattern to the numbers. When were lines of latitude and longitude invented?"

He shrugged. "We Drummonds are more into stealing history than learning about it."

"You can't fool me." Her bright gaze challenged him. Her whole face glowed with an excitement that he couldn't help feel beginning to tingle at the tips of his own fingers and toes. And some other, more private places. "You're a professional treasure hunter. I'm confident you know the histories of your wrecks better than you know what's going on in the world today."

"Is there still a world out there?" It was too much fun to torment her and watch the impatience and frustration flash in her eyes. "I try to avoid contact with it."

"Easy enough to do when you have your own island, I suppose." She shot him a glance. "But seriously, could these be latitude and longitude?"

Jack peered at the faint patterns of numbers. They did look like Roman numerals, which as far as he knew had never been used to write location coordinates. "They did use latitude and longitude in the eighteenth century, sure. They found their location using a sextant, which measured the angle of the sun to the horizon, so they could know where they were in relation to the equator, and a chronometer, which kept Greenwich Mean Time so they could figure out which time zone they were in by how far off their high noon was from London's." He let out a sigh. "Latitude around here is about twenty-six degrees—we're twenty-eight degrees north of the equator—and longitude is about eighty degrees west of London."

He peered at the painted hatch marks on the wall. They buzzed in front of his tired eyes. Then the number twenty—XX—popped out. Then VIII—the number eight. And IX—nine, then XIV—fourteen. "You might be on to something."

"Yes! Now all we have to do is write it down and find that treasure." The shine in her eyes made his stomach do a weird flip. It even made him keep his mouth shut about how it was bound to be a lot more complicated than that. For some reason he didn't want to disappoint Vicki. He wanted to make her happy.

Now, that was disturbing.

Four

Vicki sat on the prow of the boat, squinting at her pages of notes in the blazing early morning sun. Above them, thousands of cotton-ball clouds scudded across the vast sky and not one provided a lick of shade. No sleep and an army of nonsensical numbers marching through her brain had driven her half-mad.

And then there was Jack.

He was being so nice. So helpful. It was disarming and troubling. This was not the Jack she knew and loved/hated. She was beginning to think he might be up to something a lot more complicated than wanting to seduce her and dump her again.

"I still don't get what we're doing out here." He called from the deck where he was steering them… somewhere. "Those numbers don't mean anything that we can figure out."

"I hope coming out on the water will give us some perspective on the map." It had been her idea, queasy stomach and all. A flask of stomach-calming ginger tea sat by her side, and so far, so good. "It's right here in front of us somewhere. We have all the pieces. We just need to put them together."

Easier said than done, especially with the distraction of a barely clad Jack Drummond a few feet away, sun gleaming off his tanned, muscled form. She should probably just have sex with him and get it over with. That might be the only way to reduce the sexual tension pounding in the air like jungle drums.

He kept shooting sly glances at her, from beneath that dark lock of hair that dipped to his eyes. She tried to convince herself that she'd already rowed his rowboat and there was nothing to get excited about…but her memories of Jack in the sack unfortunately had the opposite effect.

Was he still the tender and passionate lover she remembered? Or had time hardened him into a more impatient or guarded bedmate? Curiosity made her skin tingle and she pulled her attention back to the stack of papers in her hand. Printed images of the ceiling fresco with its ragged coastline and wispy sprawl of Roman numerals.

They'd translated the numerals into familiar numbers as best they could, and Jack had pointed out that they weren't coordinates, at least not according to any system he knew.

They probably should have slept at that point, but the bed was covered with plaster chunks and dust and she didn't want to risk a discussion of where else they might sleep because his agreement to help her was contingent on her agreeing to join him in his bed. With her luck, they'd end up in a single bed with his chest as her pillow.

"Tired?" Jack must have seen her yawn.

"Not at all." She smiled briskly. Let him think she was a demon who didn't need sleep. "Nothing like a little sunlight and salt air to recharge my fuel cells."

"I couldn't agree more." His gruff voice held a hint of laughter. She resisted the urge to turn around because she didn't feel like being broadsided by a vision of his brawny body. "So where's the wreck?"

"It's out there somewhere."

The ocean was so vast. Opaque and impenetrable, its blue surface heaved under the boat. Maybe the wreck had been pounded to smithereens over the centuries. Or washed far out to sea in a storm. Or been found and stripped clean by one of Jack's more enterprising ancestors.

"What if it's a code?" Jack's voice jolted her from her train of depressing thoughts.

"Of course it's a code. What else could it be?" Adrenaline surged through her. Why hadn't she thought of that? She'd been so hung up on the latitude and longitude theory that it hadn't crossed her mind that the numerals had some other meaning. She peered at the pages with fresh interest, while trying to hide her sudden enthusiasm from Jack.

If the numbers were letters, there would be some that occurred more than others—*A,* for example. She scanned the pages. And sighed. Roman numerals were insanely repetitive already. Instead of having 1, 2, 3, 4, 5, 6, 7, 8, 9 and 10, they had I, II, III, IV, V, VI, VII, VIII, IX and X. A grand total of three characters: I, V and X. Her careful transcription contained no higher numbers like C for a hundred or M for a thousand. Words were hardly jumping off the page at her.

"Cracked it yet?" His teasing voice made her head jerk involuntarily in his direction.

"Almost." Great. Another eyeful of his bulging biceps as he pushed some button on the boat deck. "Maybe we should throw out a net and see if we can catch the wreck."

He chuckled. "Or maybe you're just hungry for more fish."

Her stomach lurched at the prospect. It was barely 8:00 a.m. She reached for her ginger tea and took a bracing gulp. She stared at her pages of numbers. Of course she wasn't even sure they were the right numbers. They'd tried to find gaps between the endless rows of Xs and Is and Vs and might have got some of them wrong.

There were a lot of IXs, though. And IIIs. She squinted at the page. If those corresponded to a's or o's or e's... The rolling, lurching motion of the ship was not helping her brain power. "Maybe we should go back." She needed flat, hard land under her feet to figure out this mess.

"I thought you were going to use your feminine intuition to find the wreck beneath the waves."

"It's blown a gasket. And I need an egg sandwich. Let's head into town."

"Your wish is my command." The engine roared as he swung the boat around and headed for shore at an impressive clip. She grabbed up her papers to shield them from the salt spray. She watched his steady arms for a moment.

"I do like that about boats."

"What?" He squinted in the bright sun, a half smile tugging at his mouth.

"That you can just say, let's go to town, or to the Bahamas, or Madagascar, and all you have to do is rev the engines and off you go. No roads or rules or traffic lights."

"You're beginning to understand the pull of the sea." He watched her steadily for a moment until his gaze felt as if it was going to burn a hole in her. "No speeding tickets, either."

He floored the accelerator, or whatever you called it with boats, and suddenly they seemed to be shooting across the surface of the water, bouncing hard. She grabbed a nearby chrome rail and hung on for dear life as she felt her hair unravel and stream behind her in the wind. Part of her wanted to scream, and the rest wanted to let out a whoop of joy, as cobwebs fled her mind and adrenaline shrieked to every corner of her body.

By the time they reached the shore, she'd broken a sweat just sitting still—or attempting to—and she couldn't wipe the goofy smile off her face. "You're crazy."

"Always have been, always will be."

They had breakfast at an outdoor café with the decor of a truck stop and a million-dollar view of the ocean. Vicki scribbled on her papers, making notes and trying out code possibilities.

"I can hear your brain working from here." Jack relaxed in his chair with an iced tea.

"Is the ticking keeping you awake?" She didn't glance up. Something about the pattern of the Vs made her think she was on the verge of a breakthrough.

"It's more of a humming sound, like a laser."

She met his gaze. "Careful you don't get zapped."

"I might like it." Humor danced in his eyes. He was flirting again. Worse yet, she was liking it. Where was all the hatred and bitterness she'd hoped to feel?

Don't fall for him again. He'll only get bored and dump you.

Her mind knew the truth, but her body kept rippling with pleasurable tension. His broad, arrogant mouth was so annoyingly kissable. That confident sparkle in his eye promised heights of sensual pleasure she hadn't scaled since…the last time she slept with Jack.

Sunshine and lack of sleep were making her loopy. "I need sleep, and I mean *sleep,* or I'll never figure this out."

"Paloma will have tidied up the bed by now." His feral grin sent a shiver of…warning to her toes.

"You have a housekeeper?" Hard to imagine surf-bum Jack with staff.

He shrugged. "Sometimes I'm out on the water for a week or more at a time. The lizards would take over the house if someone didn't come in and fight back the forces of nature."

"I guess that's a hazard of living in a historic property."

"Built by pirates with no construction experience." He stretched, giving her yet another annoying view of his biceps. "Amazing it hasn't fallen down by now."

"I suppose if you can figure out how to keep a wooden vessel afloat on water 365 days a year, piling some rocks into a sturdy house doesn't seem so hard. I wonder if they buried any treasure in the walls while they were building."

Jack lifted a brow. "Maybe we should start chiseling around the window frames?"

"Let's find the wreck first." She lifted her bag onto her shoulder. "After I get some sleep."

To her surprise, Jack did let her sleep, alone in the luxurious comfort of fresh white sheets. Jack's silent and invisible housekeeper had removed every trace of plaster dust and left the room sparkling and smelling pleasantly of beeswax. When Vicki awoke, sometime late that afternoon, the newly revealed fresco hovered above her like a summer sky, its colors intense, unfaded by sunbeams and time. Why had someone covered it up? They must have wanted to hide the information contained in this map. Maybe they had it committed to memory and needed to conceal it from greedy family members or servants until they found the time and means to retrieve it.

She could easily imagine the various Drummonds not trusting each other. They seemed like a pretty tormented family. Maybe there was a curse that needed to be lifted.

Speaking of which, where was Jack? Her ears pricked as she listened for sounds of him. As far as she knew, he hadn't come near while she was sleeping.

She slipped out of bed and walked over the cool tiled floors into the hallway. "Jack?" No sound of him. She really should enjoy the solitude while she had it. What was she doing trying to hunt him down and bring him back to torment her?

She climbed up on the bed with her phone. Fifteen missed calls, all from the same number. Why couldn't this jerk get the hint? She'd never even been out on a real date with him. Leo Parker had cornered her at an art opening and sweet-talked her with promises of a dinner at Nobu. The dinner was delicious, the company not so much. When he'd sidled up to her at an auction she was attending, with an invitation to dinner at Annisa, she'd found herself too hungry and impoverished to resist. It wasn't hard to make conversation with him—all you had to do was nod while he talked about himself. The tricky part was getting away from him at the end of the night.

Maybe he thought she was playing hard to get? She really shouldn't have accepted his invitation to the U.S. Open. She didn't even like tennis that much. But with money so tight and her valiant efforts to keep up appearances taking a toll, she figured it would at least give her a story to tell at all the art openings she attended nightly to eat the free hors d'oeuvres and cozy up to the rich art lovers she hoped would be her future clientele.

He'd turned into an octopus behind court number eight. Lips like raw fish and arms of steel. She'd managed to fend him off with a sudden coughing fit and threats of a virulent sore throat, but since then he'd called at least once a day. Staying at Sinclair's house on Long Island had kept him at bay, and she'd assumed coming to Florida would lose him for good.

Most people would have taken a hint by now. That he hadn't was troubling.

Reluctantly, she listened to his plea. "Hey, babe, haven't seen you around lately. We could catch the new *South Pacific* and go out for a late bite…." He droned on. Grrr. If only he was charming and handsome. Or at least one of those. And she didn't like musicals, either.

You led him on. She could hear her friends' accusatory voices in her head, even though she hadn't told any of them about him. Maybe she was embarrassed to stoop so low for a free meal. And now she was here leading Jack Drummond on for the chance to win a reward that would once have been pocket change to her.

Did this make her a strumpet? It probably would if she was actually sleeping with them. Or even kissing them. She shuddered at the memory of Leo's cold, wet, sloppy attempt. A fumble from Jack, though...

She let out a sigh and deleted the rest of her messages. Nothing important. Life was happening back in New York as usual. The rich getting richer, the poor getting screwed out of what little money they had. She couldn't wait to work her way back into the former group. Which was the *only* reason why she was here right now.

Where was Jack? She headed out to look again. The sunset blazed through the kitchen windows, casting a mellow golden light over the expensively refurbished stone counters and the huge industrial appliances. Lights had come on in the hallways—subtle sconces embedded in the limestone walls—but that seemed to happen by magic or automation. "Hey, Jack. Where the heck are you?"

No answer. She cruised through the living room where a pair of patio doors stood open to the outside, no screen. No wonder he had lizards on his ceiling. Outside the open doors the salt tang of the sea greeted her and a breeze whipped her hair, but there was no sign of her host.

Barefoot, she picked her way over the prickly grass and down some stone steps to the dock nearest the house. His boat was gone. He'd abandoned her here on this island in the middle of nowhere.

Suddenly, the golden fingers of sunset, spreading across the dark, still, ocean, looked downright spooky. She glanced over her shoulder. What was she expecting? The ghost of a peg-legged pirate? She sucked in a breath and suppressed a shudder.

Jack was probably in the arms of some well-stacked barmaid, like all his salt-caked predecessors. What did she care? She only wanted him for his expertise, so the quicker she could get out of here, the better.

She went back to the map and stared at it, her stomach growling. There were a lot of numbers, but none of them very high. In fact she hadn't seen a number higher than twenty-five.

An idea flashed into her mind. If each number corresponded to the place of a letter in the alphabet—if III was the letter *C,* say, and VII was the letter *G…*

Frantically, she grabbed a fresh sheet of notepaper, then scrolled back and forth through the alphabet, translating the numbers again using this new system. Slowly and painstakingly, a message from the past emerged on the crumpled sheet of paper in front of her.

Start at dawne and rouwe due north from Deade Men's Cowve to the baneyan tree. Set course east northeast and row ye three score strokes. Swing thy prouwe to the horizon and row five score strokes towarde the sunne, where the north spalle of the island meets Raster's Docke. Keepe them close as ye row seven score strokes east southeast. Hold thy oar alofte at noone and it shall point to that which ye seek forty fathoms belowe.

* * *

When she reached the end, she stared at the paper and let out a long exhale. She felt like leaping into the air…for a split second. Then she realized how insubstantial the directions actually were. Dependent on the position of the sun and the angles of the boat to the shore, they might not yield the same results at all after three hundred years of geologic change.

On the other hand…

How could Jack abandon her like this? She climbed off the bed and made her way to the kitchen, where she managed to forage together a turkey wrap so he wouldn't return to find her bleached bones on his patio. Three score strokes. A score was twenty, so three score was sixty. But surely strokes by a big man would be different than strokes by a scrawny cabin boy, and how would she know which was right?

Let's just assume Jack's ancestors all looked exactly like him. Burly, brawny and badass. She sighed. She needed Jack and a rowboat. And he was busy under a barmaid.

She couldn't wait until she was independent and didn't have to depend on anybody for anything.

It was nearly dawn when she heard the sound of a boat engine in the distance. She wondered whether to pretend she'd been asleep the whole time and hadn't noticed he was gone, then decided she couldn't be bothered. Instead, she marched to the dock and waited there in the moonlight with her hands on her hips like a neglected wife.

He watched her from the deck. "Nice to be welcomed home by a beautiful woman."

"I'm glad you came home. I thought I might be marooned here forever if you got hit by a bus."

"I don't think there's been a bus near here since the 1960s."

"What a relief. And I cracked the code. Now all we have to do is go dig up the loot."

Still in the boat, a cardboard box in his arms, he paused. "Where is it?"

"Under the sea, of course. Off a spall and three score strokes here and there. We'll find it." And she turned and marched back to the house, hoping her backside looked sexier than his barmaid's.

"I went to visit a friend." He put some items in the fridge from the box he'd brought in.

"That's what I figured."

"Not that kind of friend." He looked amused. "Were you jealous?"

Embarrassed that her voice or face had apparently given too much away, she only risked a shrug. "It's your life."

"My friend is an old fisherman who's been catching dolphin and sea bass off these shores for fifty years."

"Dolphin? That's disgusting."

He laughed. "What we call dolphin is what you Northerners call mahimahi. It's a fish that swims with the dolphins."

"Well, that's clear as clam chowder." She crossed her arms over her chest again, not at all sure if she believed the fisherman part. "Did you stay up all night singing sea shanties?"

"I wanted to ask him if he'd ever seen traces of the wreck or bits of spar that could be from it. He said he never has."

"How encouraging."

"It might be. If it's buried beneath the sand or locked into encrusted coral it might be more or less intact—missing cup parts and all."

"Except that we'll never find it."

He poured himself a big glass of orange juice and swigged it, his Adam's apple throbbing rhythmically. She tugged her eyes from the sight of his powerful hand holding the glass. She needed that hand to tug on some oars. "Not without my cannons, no."

"Cannons? You're going to lob cannonballs into the surf?"

"Nope. These are high-tech treasure hunting cannons. They blow air with force and rip holes in the seabed, exposing all the goodies hidden under it."

"Boys and their toys. And how many hours did it take you to find out that your friend hadn't seen anything floating in the water?" She instantly regretted her pathetically catty question.

Jack grinned. "I like it when you're jealous. I see sparks flashing in those mystical eyes of yours. Gets me going."

"I hate you."

One brow lifted slightly. "Getting better all the time. I'll have to stay away longer next time."

"I'll swim ashore."

"I bet you would." That annoying twinkle of humor lit his face. "And you'll have to take these with you." He pulled a big stack of papers out of the cardboard box. "It appears you had some mail forwarded."

She felt her face heat. "I needed to send it somewhere. I used your address because I wasn't sure where I was going to stay."

"Or because you knew you were going to stay with me."

"Nonsense. But I did come down here to see you, and I figured you wouldn't mind." This was getting worse and worse. She didn't want to admit that she literally had no fixed address now. Her mail and subscriptions followed her like a pack of stray dogs behind a gypsy camp.

He riffled through her morning papers. "The *Wall Street Journal?* The *New York Post* and *Women's Wear Daily?*"

"Just trying to keep abreast of certain trends." The lifestyles of New York's rich and famous, to be precise.

"Most people would use the internet."

"I'm traditional in some ways. I like to get newsprint on my fingers while I enjoy my morning coffee."

He laughed. "You're an old-fashioned girl in many ways, Vicki. One more thing to love about you."

She tried to look steely and unconcerned as she took her papers from him. She'd kept her familiar subscriptions going through her first couple of moves, assuming she'd soon be settled. Once she knew the routine it was easy enough to arrange for them to follow her on her travels. They were a turtle shell of familiarity in her ever-shifting and far-too-mobile world and she hated to start the day without them. Already she was dying to flip to Page Six and see if anything about Sinclair Drummond and his new fiancée, Annie, had crossed the pages. If she did one good deed in her lifetime, it was forcing those two to see they were meant for each other.

"Do you want to hear what the map says or not?" He didn't seem to care one way or the other.

"Sure. Mushroom omelet?"

"Why not." She pulled a folded paper from the pocket of her pants. "Here's what your crusty old ancestor wrote." She looked up, and was further annoyed to see Jack pulling out a pan and retrieving ingredients from the fridge instead of riveting his attention to her words. As she read, though, he turned and frowned with gratifying concentration.

"What the heck is a spall?" he said, after a long pause.

"I looked it up. A spall is something that has broken off. So maybe a little chunk of land off the end of the island?"

"There isn't one."

"Maybe it's under the sea now." Why was he arguing with her over this minor point? "More importantly, where's Dead Men's Cove?"

"Thataway." He tilted his head toward the fridge. "I found another skeleton embedded in the rocks there the other day. The old family story was that shipwreck victims were washed into the cove by the current. I now suspect it's where they buried their enemies."

She shivered. "Lovely people, your ancestors."

He dropped quivering raw egg onto the bubbling oil, and she watched as it hardened into a solid, golden mass. "We're a proud and solitary race, who don't take well to interlopers." He winked.

"I'd better watch my back, then." She dragged her eyes from his once again. His wink had sent a little frisson of sensation darting across her midsection. Which was ridiculous. She distracted herself by pulling plates from a shelf and hunting around for cutlery. "What about Raster's Dock?"

"Whatever it is, it's long gone. There was an old

homestead just up the coast with a spit of rock, like a jetty, in front of it. Maybe we'll assume it's there for the sake of argument."

"Do you have a rowboat?"

"Several score of them." He grinned. "How many is in a score anyway? I'm guessing you looked it up."

"Twenty." She glanced out the window. "We'd better hurry if we're going to make it by dawn."

"Don't worry. We have another forty-five minutes. We're a lot closer to the equator down here than you're used to. Dawn doesn't wake you up in the middle of the night, even in summer."

She took her plate, now freshly decorated with half the omelet, and dug her fork right into it. She was glad she'd managed to avoid another night in Jack's bed. She was beginning to think it could be far too risky to enjoy his charms. They might have the same effect as "just one drink" on a former alcoholic. "Let's hurry."

Five

Jack's broad back flexed in the light from the electric lantern as they tugged the rowboat from its dusty grave in the disused boathouse. Nets and buoys and fishing rods of every size and description lined the walls and crisscrossed the sandy floor.

Vicki tried not to break a nail as she helped him lift it over an old crate filled with tangled rope. "When did someone last use this, 1964?" The rowboat was an indeterminate color, somewhere between beige and pink. "And what makes you think it will still hold water?"

"She's a trusty one. I use her all the time."

"That's not what this layer of dust is trying to tell me. When would you ever need to row somewhere?"

"When I don't want anyone to hear me coming." He turned back to her and shot her a sly grin.

Which made her stomach do a crazy flip.

She grabbed one end of the boat and peered into its depths. "Great. This is your sneaking-up-on-unsuspecting-maidens craft. I hope there aren't too many condom wrappers in the bottom."

He chuckled. "Nope. Don't see any. Maybe we'll have to put a couple in there."

He didn't turn around to see her faux-shocked expression. "In your fantasies, Jack Drummond."

"Indeed." He hoisted his side of the boat higher, no doubt to further unhinge her with the sight of his powerful physique. "A man's allowed his dreams. One of the few rights and privileges no one can take away from us."

"Hmm, you're right. I'm surprised there isn't a tax on steamy male imaginings."

Now she had an eyeful of his burly chest as he walked backward—without looking, she could tell his eyes were entirely on her—out of the old boathouse and down onto the beach.

She tried to glance past him, out to where the sky was brightening every second, even though the sun hadn't peeked over the horizon yet. "How long will it take us to row to Dead Men's Cove?"

"About three minutes, once we're afloat. It's pretty calm today."

They shoved the boat out into the water and carefully climbed in while it rocked in the quiet surf. Her feet were bare and the bottom of the boat felt dusty and splintery. Jack rowed and she sat up in the bow, trying to remember the words she'd written down as it wasn't yet light enough to read.

"This is Dead Men's Cove," said Jack quietly, as they rounded a small spit of land just as the first white-hot sliver of sun peeked over the horizon.

"Row due north from Dead Men's Cove to the banyan tree. Where's the banyan tree?"

Jack tilted his head back the way they came. Vicki looked through the predawn gloom to see a huge, gnarled tree rising above the sea grape near the beach. "Let's go."

He swung the boat around with minimal effort, bare chest shimmering gold in the first rays of sun. Couldn't he have worn a shirt? This was distracting and she needed to focus all her attention on following the details of the directions. "How old is that tree?"

"Dunno. Been there almost forever, I guess." His muscles contracted and released as he pulled on the oars, sending powerful ripples across his hard belly. She tugged her focus to the spreading branches of the tree again, but her gaze shifted inexorably back to the vision of his strong body at work. Apparently, she had been manless for too long.

"When we get to the tree, you row east-northeast."

"The tree is inland." He glanced over his shoulder at it.

"Go as close as you can get and then turn."

His broad hands gripped the oars with force. Why was she paying attention to his hands at a time like this? They had only a few minutes to find the location before the sun would be in the wrong place until tomorrow. "How do you know which way east-northeast is?"

He chuckled. "In my blood."

"You probably have a compass somewhere near your solar plexus." She glanced at it for a moment—flat, hard stomach, beaded with trickles of sweat—then looked hard at the horizon. She could see a boat in the distance, and another farther to the south. She wondered if any of them could guess their strange changes of direction were due to three-hundred-year-old instructions.

As they neared the rocky coastline by the tree, he swung the boat around ninety degrees and rowed farther out into the ocean. "One, two, three…" Sixty strokes. She kept count, glad of something to do while Jack put his entire body weight into propelling the rowboat through the shining water. "Sixty. Now row toward the horizon."

With little visible effort, Jack swiveled the boat again and started pulling for the dividing line between sea and sky. Again she counted, this time to one hundred, the words beating an eerie rhythm with the splashing of the oars, out in the quiet world of the open sea.

She peered back at the shore. *To where the north spalle of the island abuts Raster's Docke.* The end of the island was cloaked in trees right to the water. The shoreline behind it looked similarly featureless. Was this where their quest would end? "Eighty, eighty-one, eighty-two…" She kept the count going, staring at the island, looking for a sign, for anything. There was no spall and no dock, with or without extra *e*'s. "Ninety-nine, one hundred. Stop!"

Jack brought the boat to an impressive stop by spinning it in place. "We're supposed to be at the place where the north spall of the island abuts Raster's Dock, but were out in the middle of nowhere."

He squinted at the coastline. "Those rocks there, you can barely see them now, but at high tide they're exposed and look like the remains of a jetty. I'll bet anything that's Raster's Dock. Don't know about the spall, though. There's nothing under the ocean there.

If there was, I'd have run aground on it at some point when I was a kid."

"Damn." Vicki chewed her lip and glanced about. "We're obviously supposed to stare at how they line up as you row east-southeast."

"What if the spall isn't a spall anymore, but is part of the island? It could have been built up by sand shifting in a storm." Jack stared hard at the wooded tree canopy. "Never bothered crashing my way in there, though, so I don't know."

"Let's pretend it is and give it a try." The end of the island didn't quite line up with where the rocks started. "I think we need to shift thataway a bit." She jerked her chin to the right.

"North-northeast, ma'am. I'm on it." Jack smoothly turned the boat and pulled at the oars. "I see it. Look at those tall trees—or trees on taller land—now they're lining up with where I know the rocks are. What next?"

"Don't pretend you don't remember! *Keep them close as ye row seven score strokes east-southeast.* That's one hundred and forty." She didn't have to tell him to hurry. He'd already shifted the boat and pulled hard on the oars, and the boat seemed to leap across the water at his touch. Timing was crucial. A minute too late and the sun would be in the wrong place as it hit the oar to point to the shipwreck.

"One thirty-nine… One forty!" He spun the boat again to stop its forward momentum, sending her lurching against the hard wood. "Hold up an oar."

Jack hoisted the dripping piece of wood into the air, bracing it with his arms against the bottom of the boat. Its long black shadow pointed right at Vicki, making her scoot to the side, rocking the boat. With her out of the way, it tapered over the edge of the boat and pointed its long dark finger toward the land.

"Do you suppose that means it's right here?" Vicki peered into the murky depths over the side. Deep and dark, the ocean revealed no secrets.

"Unless they're playing a joke and it's actually buried on the island." Jack peered at the now-distant palm-fringed shore. "We've never looked right here, though. The other map said it was about half a mile to the south." His face wore an expression of intense concentration mingled with barely controlled excitement. "There's something compelling about the way it uses points on shore to line us up. It feels like the way a seaman would think."

Vicki glanced about. Nothing but shimmering ocean in every direction. "How do we mark our position so we can find it again? We can't exactly plunge a stake in."

He pulled a black contraption from his pocket. "GPS. I'll plug in our coordinates." His fingers worked the buttons. "We could mark it with a buoy, but no need to put a big shiny X on the spot for everyone else to see."

"I like the way you think, Cap'n Jack."

His quick grin caused her blood to heat. Or maybe it was just excitement that they might be right over the wreck of the sunken ship. "Do you think there are skeletons down there?"

"Undoubtedly." His grin broadened with a hint of menace. "How are your scuba skills?"

"Rusty." She didn't like breathing underwater at the best of times, but especially not if she was sharing space with a bunch of barnacle-covered dead pirates.

"Maybe we should forget the whole thing and go lie

on the beach." He peered at her under a lock of sun-streaked brown hair.

"No way!" She shoved him slightly, causing the boat to rock, and both of them to laugh. "I'm afraid to leave, though, in case we can't find our way back to this spot."

"Don't worry. I have it programmed into my seafaring brain as well as my GPS. I could find my way here in the dark. Let's go back and get the gear."

Jack rowed back to shore, describing the moment he'd found the last wreck he'd pillaged. How they'd seen one end of an anchor poking out of the seabed, then the encrusted end of an old cannon. It wasn't until they were back on dry land that Vicki realized she'd never even thought about being seasick.

They returned under the steam of Jack's powerful outboard motor, carrying scuba diving gear. When they reached the spot indicated by the directions in the fresco, Jack killed the engines. "Let's look around."

"We just jump right in?" She peered into the murky, featureless depths.

"Nope. We'll let the sonar do that for us." He lowered a line over the side of the boat, bearing a piece of equipment he called a towfish. "Now we trawl along real slow and look for something interesting." Up on the bridge, they stared at a wishy-washy black-and-white picture on a monitor as the boat moved. Vicki stared at the screen, but to her, it all looked like a bowl of undersea oatmeal.

"Hold up." Jack peered at the image. "Something's down here."

"That was easy."

"Don't get cocky. It could be an old car." He maneuvered the boat around. "Let's go in for a closer look." Vicki squinted at the wavering gray image, willing it to be the shattered remains of a great wooden vessel. Jack punched buttons and moved with effortless calm to bring the boat around while scanning the surrounding area. "Can't see much, but in my experience the distention of the surface makes it worth exploring."

"What does that mean in English?"

"It's bumpy, so there might be something under the sand."

"Let's get our shovels and pails and get to work."

"My sentiments exactly, but don't dive in just yet." He swung down from the bridge and strode to the rear of the boat, where he maneuvered two big cylinders down into the water. "These will blow the prop wash down onto the sand, and hopefully move it, so we can get a better look at what's under there." The engine roared and the water around the boat turned murky with churned-up sand as their wake streamed down the tubes.

"How are we supposed to see anything in this water?"

"We have to wait for the sand to settle." He winked.

"Won't it cover everything up again?"

"Maybe." He switched off the engine, then with a pleasant smile he stretched out on the deck, torturing her with the sight of his chiseled chest. Why couldn't they be somewhere cold and miserable so he'd have to don a wetsuit? She turned the other way to distract herself. She'd worn dark sunglasses so she could stare right at him without his knowing, and the aftereffects of a morning's ogling were wreaking havoc on her sanity.

A sleek white vessel sat still in the water out toward the horizon. "Is that a fishing boat?"

"Sometimes." He hadn't even looked. "Sometimes it's a party boat. Owned by Iago Knoll."

"The corporate raider? What's he doing down here?" She squinted at the boat, looking for the tall, arrogant silhouette she knew well from New York.

"Same as everyone else. Looking for some fun in the sun."

"That's not what I'm doing here." She crossed her arms over her chest, which was covered in SPF 50 sun-block and a T-shirt over her swimsuit.

"Not yet." He flashed that wicked grin at her again. "But we'll give you time."

"No way. I'm far too much of a New Yorker to enjoy lazing around in the sun."

His deft fingers checked the connections on his scuba equipment. "Who said anything about lazing? Surfing, sailing, kayaking, deep-sea fishing—no need to be a deck-chair potato down here."

"Sounds exhausting. I'd rather be pounding some hot pavement." She jerked her eyes from his hands to her own scuba equipment. Jack had already checked it over and she trusted his judgment more than her own. "All this sun and salt air is making me dizzy." *And you're not helping.* The water around the boat was clearing. "How long until we can jump in?"

"Anytime you like. Sometimes it's fun to be down there as the mist of sand recedes and reveals what you're looking for."

"A cup base sticking up out of the sand like Excali-bur."

"You think it's the base?"

"It's not the stem because Sinclair has that. So it's either the cup—the most exciting part, and probably the easiest to find—or the base. So I'm guessing it's the base."

"Calculated pessimism. That was never your style." He heaved his tanks onto his back.

"I've learned from experience."

"Apparently you've been having the wrong experiences." He peered over the edge of the boat. "The sand is settling."

"I'm going in." Might as well get the first dive over with before she lost her nerve.

"Go for it."

The warm, eerie silence of the underwater world enveloped Vicki as she plunged beneath the surface. Her flippers propelled her lower, and she reminded herself that it was okay to breathe. She heard, or rather felt, the impact as Jack slid into the water behind her, flipped and dived for the seabed.

The sun above brightened the water, and she looked around, trying to gain her bearings in Neptune's unfamiliar kingdom. But she needed to go down into the murky depths where the sun barely filtered through the water. She held a flashlight in one hand, and a pointed steel rod in the other. Jack said that was the best tool for rooting about in the sand. She supposed it would also work as a deadly weapon should the need arise.

He had a metal detector and something that looked like a claw, and he was already a good ten yards below her. She pumped her legs trying to keep up, as she didn't fancy being lost and alone down here in this blue underworld. Jack's strong thighs powered him effortlessly through the water, but she was almost panting into her respirator by the time she neared the ocean floor. He scanned the sand with the detector, and she peered around for a place to start poking her ridiculous stick.

The propeller wash had carved out a shallow irregular bowl in the sand, and as her eyes accustomed to the dim light—and she figured out how to turn on her flashlight in underwater slow motion—she saw an item over to the left of the indentation.

Must be the cup base, she teased herself. Down here in the vast, dark water, the idea of finding one single three-hundred-year-old artifact seemed ludicrous. She'd anticipated a little rummaging in Jack's attics and then her work would be done. This situation had spiraled right out of control.

She approached the object and poked around it gently with her stick. It didn't budge, and with a little determined burrowing she discovered that it was large and the rest was buried beneath the surface. The mysterious item was encrusted with barnacles or other sea life, but there was definitely something solid underneath them. Probably a 1967 Chevy.

She flashed her light at Jack in the agreed-upon signal and he swam over. He ran his metal detector over the object a number of times, then turned and gave her a thumbs-up.

If only she'd learned American Sign Language when she had the chance. They dug around together and the more they dug, the deeper the object got until Jack gave her the signal to surface.

Rushing toward the light felt like coming back to life after a sojourn in the underworld. Once afloat, she pulled up her mask and took off her respirator. Jack popped up beside her and pushed his respirator aside to reveal a big grin. "Damn, girl, you're a magic charm!"

"You think this is it?"

"It's a cannon."

"How can you tell?"

"See one, you've seen them all. Looks like the right era, too. I think you've finally found the lost treasure of Macassar Drummond."

Maybe it was the excitement shining in his eyes or maybe it was the scuba gear, but he suddenly looked exactly like the Jack Drummond who'd stolen her heart and left it in pieces. She struggled to ignore the mess of sensations running rampant inside her—while staying afloat in the water by paddling her flippers. "It's a shame you have such a boring name when your ancestors have such good ones."

He grinned. "Isn't it? I'm going to make sure my son has a name you can really hang your hat on."

"How can you be sure you'll have a boy?"

"The Drummonds always have a boy. That's why we're still here. If we had girls they wouldn't be Drummonds." He seemed to float effortlessly in the water despite the heavy tanks.

She wished she could turn and stride smoothly away, but that wasn't going to happen. "Guess there's too much testosterone in the Drummond blood."

"Too much something, for sure." The sun gleamed off his bronzed face. "But maybe you're about to find the cup and change all that. Let's get back on deck and do some more digging electronically."

He went back to the sonar and used something called a magnetometer to zero in on places to dig. There were several pockets of matter that showed up on the equipment, begging to be investigated. They dived again and turned up two broken glass bottles and an almost-intact plate, all encrusted with sea life but clearly recognizable.

"My God, we've found it, haven't we?" Vicki gasped for air as they surfaced again. The sun was setting behind them over the land, casting its burnished glow over the sea.

"You found it, babe. I'd never have done it without you. That map would have stayed hidden up there for another two hundred years or more if you hadn't had the bright idea to chisel away at the ceiling above my bed."

They climbed back on the deck. Jack was too excited to go back to the house. He insisted on making dinner on the boat so he could dive by moonlight overnight. Vicki protested until he showed her the cornucopia of goodies inside his fridge. After a dinner of chilled shrimp with mango salsa and coconut rice, they sipped Jack's special "diver cocktail" made of pomegranate, orange and lemon juice. She suggested that because she certainly wasn't heading to the briny depths in the dark, she should be allowed a cold beer, but he explained that because alcohol and diving didn't mix, he didn't allow booze on board.

So she couldn't even blame alcohol for what happened next.

Six

"Damn, I didn't realize how much I've missed you." Jack lolled against a floatation device on the deck. Water drops still glistened on his tanned stomach, although his high-tech trunks looked dry.

The moon cast a lazy silver glow over the whole scene and the warm evening air caressed Vicki like a hug. Which wasn't helpful because she was already battling a sensual languor at the end of their long, high-octane day. "You missed being bossed around by a crazy broad?"

"Sure, who wouldn't?" His lips cracked to reveal those ridiculously white teeth. "And when she's as crazy beautiful as you, it's impossible to resist obeying her commands."

"What if I command you to take us to Monte Carlo?"

"I'd be delighted." His sleepy gaze challenged her. "Though we might run out of fuel on the way."

"Excuses, excuses. What do you do for fun, Jack Drummond?"

"I'm doing it right now. Lazing on my beloved boat with the woman of my dreams."

She laughed, but his words plucked at some long-forgotten string inside her. Then she reminded herself he was just teasing her. "With treasure sparkling away hidden in the sands below us."

"It doesn't get any better than this."

"I guess you're an easy man to please."

"Or I've managed to organize the perfect life for me."

She envied his contentment, and damn, it made him attractive, too. "I intend to organize the perfect life for me when I get back to New York." She could already picture her apartment, maybe with a view of the water or of Central Park, once she made her first few big deals. Well-heeled clients would visit her tastefully decorated pad to discuss trophy items they needed to add to their collections—a Matisse, perhaps, or a small Rodin for the garden.

Jack jolted her from her thoughts by lifting himself from the deck and joining her on the deep, upholstered bench with its view over the silvery water. The skin of her thigh sizzled slightly as he sat down right next to her. "So why aren't you there right now, making your dreams come true?"

"I need to find the cup first."

"I know you're trying to convince me that you're hell-bent on saving the Drummonds from a future of misery, but I don't think you're that charitable. You told me you want the reward, but it's small change in the grand scheme. Unless you really, really need that small amount of money for some reason." His eyes narrowed and he leaned toward her.

Her stomach clenched, partly at the ugly realization that he now suspected she was strapped for cash, but mostly at the blood-heating closeness of him.

"I know your dad died, and I'm sorry."

"Thanks." She was getting more flustered by the minute. This was way too personal.

"But that should mean—and I apologize for being crude—that you'd be rolling in it by now. Did something happen to the family war chest?"

Vicki's mouth was stuck half-open. No one knew about her personal financial ruin. Nobody. All the lost money had been hidden in an offshore interest, which made it impossible to prove or claim back once it had been swindled away. She'd spent the past eighteen months hustling to maintain the friendships and contacts she had without letting them know she was living from hand to mouth.

"You're very quiet, Vicki Sin-cere. I'm beginning to suspect that you're flat broke." His eyes twinkled with a mixture of amusement and genuine concern that ate at her insides like acid.

What could she say now? She couldn't lie to Jack. He'd see right through her and laugh his ass off.

So she leaned in—it was only a few inches—and covered his taunting mouth with her own. Their lips locked instantly, and a rush of fevered confusion, desire and long-forgotten passion roared through her like a flash flood. Her arms wound around him, and she felt his hands sliding around her waist, pulling her close.

A sigh fled her mouth, into his, and she couldn't stop

it. She couldn't stop the kiss either. It took on a life of its own, powering her entire body, as she reeled from the force of his desire striking hers and making sparks that rained down over both of them.

Her nipples thickened beneath her swimsuit and goose bumps flashed over her thighs. She clung to him, inhaling the fabulous scent of Jack Drummond—sea, salt air and that indefinable dash of raw healthy male that made him utterly irresistible.

Their kiss deepened and she found herself sitting in his lap, lips still locked to his. His big hands squeezed her backside, making her squirm with pleasure. Her chest rubbed against his, her hard nipples rasping against his washboard abs and sending hot flames of arousal leaping through her. He tasted like heaven, rich and warm and oh so familiar. The years since their last kiss evaporated as if they'd never happened.

As if she'd never said *I love you* and ruined everything.

That thought stilled her tongue inside his mouth and sent a stark clarity shooting through her brain. She pulled back just enough for their lips to part, which felt agonizingly painful.

"Hot damn," murmured Jack, once her mouth cleared his. "I've missed you even more than I thought."

Me, too. She managed not to say it. All these unsaid words must be building up inside her like a dam about to burst.

His rock-hard erection jutted against her thigh, and she looked down at it and laughed, glad of the distraction from her roiling emotions. "I guess you are happy to see me."

"Happy to hold on to you, as well." His arms were

still around her, and he hugged her gently, affection-
ately. Her heart did a double backflip and she closed
her eyes to avoid his gaze.

"I guess I must be getting loopy from lack of sleep
or something." She pretended to stretch. Jack's lips
touched hers, sparking an electric pulse of passion
which made her eyes jump open.

Sure enough his dark, penetrating gaze was fixed
right on her. "Believe me, sleep is the very last thing
I have on my mind right now." His wicked, predatory
grin stretched across his handsome face.

Desire flared deep inside her, hot and low, like the
rumblings of an underground geyser. Could it really
hurt that much to have a quickie with Jack? They were
both here in the middle of nowhere. They were prac-
tically naked already. And let's face it, they'd done it
before and it was really, really good.

She couldn't kid herself, right at this moment, that
having sex with Jack Drummond would do anything
at all to get him out of her system. It was likely to have
the opposite effect.

On the other hand, she was a grown-up now, with
responsibilities and pressures and a life to get back to,
not some foolish girl with too much time on her hands.

Worst-case scenario—she'd be filled with regret and
have to nurse a broken heart for a few months. Right
now that seemed worth it.

She licked his lips like the top of an ice-cream cone.
His grin widened. He licked back, and the tickling sensation reached deep inside her, to her feminine core. He
let out a low growl, like a curious puma, which made
her smile and only aroused her more. "I feel like I'm
relapsing into an old addiction."

"And there's no cure."

She didn't have to voice her agreement. Her body said it all. Her fingers explored the contours of his chest and stomach as he peeled her swimsuit away. The warm evening air caressed her bare breasts, closely followed by Jack's hungry mouth. She sighed and arched her back as he licked her nipple to a tight peak.

The stubble of his chin tickled her skin, increasing the amount of sensation building all over her. As he rose to kiss her mouth again, she ran her fingers through his thick hair, pulling him closer and kissing him with six years of pent-up passion.

The chemistry between them was explosive as always. One glance at Jack and her self-control headed for the nearest exit. One touch and she was lost. The feel of his arms around her released the tension she'd been carrying around like a shield and she sensed herself falling out of reality and into the private world they'd always shared.

She was dimly aware of the ocean around them, its gentle swells lapping around the edges of the boat. She could feel the warm evening air crowding around her, humid and sensual, caressing her body like a soft blanket, even as Jack eased her swimsuit down over her legs leaving her stark naked on the upholstered bench.

She opened her eyes enough to tug at his boxers, then opened them wider to enjoy the view as she pulled them down over his hair-roughened thighs. His arousal was unmistakable, bold and proud like everything else about him. Their eyes met and they laughed, both naked and insanely turned on, with only the big, pale moon as a witness.

They were both standing now, and Jack stepped toward her slowly, drinking in her body with his eyes as if it was the last sip of fresh water left on a long ocean voyage. He settled his hands on her hips, claiming her. His fierce kiss almost shook the breath from her body. She flung her arms around his neck and cleaved herself to him, skin to skin, from her lips down to her toes.

Her insides quivered and throbbed, already anticipating the feel of him inside her. His thick erection pressed against her belly, teasing and tormenting her with the pleasure that lay ahead. Just when she thought she couldn't stand it any longer, he lifted her onto the bench and moved over her.

He stroked her hair and murmured her name as he entered her. She lifted her hips as he filled her, drawing him deeper. "Oh, Jack." His name escaped her lips as she welcomed him back into her body, into her heart. She'd never met another man who moved her the way Jack did. All her beaus since had been a pale second best and her romantic encounters lackluster and unsatisfying. After Jack Drummond, every other man seemed a wan shadow whose petty needs and foolish conversation bored her.

Jack always managed to reach right into her core and wake her right up. She let out a moan of raw passion as he touched a place deep inside her that hadn't known feeling or sensation since she last saw him. She writhed underneath him, letting herself fly into a realm of passion she'd almost forgotten.

I love you, Jack. The ghost words haunted her, driven by memories of that passionate era in her life all those years ago. She knew she couldn't love him now. Too much water had flowed under the bridge and they were both different people with different agendas. Still, the thought swirled around her head as they moved together in a hypnotic rhythm.

His big, warm body wrapped around hers and made her feel fabulously safe and protected, although even now she knew she should feel the opposite. Jack Drummond had always been her danger zone, the place where she easily waded out of her depth and into unknown territory. He was the rock upon which her heart ran aground and became beached, only to survive scarred and damaged.

Those thoughts popped up in her brain like tiny clouds in the blue sky of a perfect sunny day. Like those passing clouds they didn't cast even the smallest shadow on her intense enjoyment of making love with Jack. Somehow it was soothing, a kind of release, to know she was getting in over her head. She'd trod so carefully in her life lately, been so afraid of making mistakes and revealing too much. At least now she knew she was hurling herself headfirst into trouble and, dammit, she was going to enjoy every sweet, soul-wringing second of it.

They moved together like a seasoned pair of dancers executing a spectacular routine they'd built and practiced together, adding new flourishes that gave each twist and turn a touch of unexpected magic. Her first climax led almost seamlessly to a second, and then a third, as she and Jack scaled new peaks of unimaginable pleasure on almost every surface in the boat. When they finally lay in each other's arms, spent, sweaty and unbelievably satisfied, she could barely believe she was still on the same planet she'd inhabited as the nervous, secretive and edgy Vicki she'd been earlier that day.

Perhaps it made a difference that she'd left the predictable solidity of dry land behind and now floated on the vast, wide ocean. She hadn't felt a trace of sea-sickness. Apparently her sea legs—or were they flippers?—had kicked in. But the real change was allowing herself to open up to Jack, physically at least, and step back into the exotic world of pleasure and passion they'd always shared.

"Vicki, Vicki, Vicki." Jack rasped her name with his last ounce of strength. "I'm beginning to remember why I ran away from you."

"Oh, yeah?" She lay propped up on one elbow. Tendrils of dark, damp hair clung to her face, which the sun had already started to work its golden magic on. "Getting bored already?" Defiance flashed in those violet eyes, challenging him.

"Not bored, no. Never bored." Thoughts were hard to come by in his present state. Especially with Vicki's long, lithe body stretched out on the padded bench in front of him, clothed only in pale moonlight. "Overwhelmed, maybe."

Vicki wasn't like other women. Once she fixed those piercing pale eyes on you, or slid those slender fingers into your hair, or maybe even glanced at you the right way from across the room, you were done for. Or he was anyway.

He drew in a long breath and watched his chest rise. His body felt as if it belonged to someone else. He himself was floating somewhere about three feet above it in a fog of sensual and sexual bliss. And they weren't even touching anymore.

"You have magical powers." He met her bright gaze.

"I wish."

"You must. How else could you find a lost ship that my ancestors, and a whole host of other people, have been hunting for centuries? And in less than a day."

"Fresh eyes."

"Yours certainly are fresh, and an intriguing shade of pale mauve, but that doesn't explain their perceptive powers."

She licked her lips, sending a shot of sensation to his groin that almost blinded him. "When you look at something every day, you don't really see it. You've been sleeping under that fresco for so long that it's just a ceiling to you. I had to stare at it for a while, and get lucky with the way the light was hitting it, and I could see that the surface wasn't entirely stable. Frescos should last a thousand years or more, but only if they're applied the right way, with the artist painting into fresh wet plaster. Yours was faded and flaking, so I thought it was worth a second look."

"I doubt a scurvy pirate worried much about the archival quality of his work. It could have just been done badly. How did you know there was another painting underneath?"

"You'd be surprised at how often there's another painting underneath the ones that pass through the hands of auctioneers and galleries. Like pirates, artists are a bunch of penniless scavengers forced to make do with what they can lay their hands on." She smiled that seductive, almost-feline smile that sent his blood pressure into overdrive. "And my hunch turned out to be a lucky one. Anyone could have figured it out, if they had a chance to look at the fresco, but your ancestors were clever enough to hide it away where only their most intimate companions would see it."

"If my forbears had spent their nights with cleverer women, they'd have found the ship and its treasure long ago."

"I shudder to think who or what your ancestors were sleeping with." Her eyes twinkled with humor. "Have any of them ever left this island for good?"

"My dad, but that was by judicial edict, not choice. He'd already gambled or drunk everything else away so it was the last thing he had left to hand over to my mom when they divorced."

"Where does your mom live now?"

"Miami." He smiled. "South Beach. She and her new husband enjoy parties more than hunting for pirate booty."

"Lucky her. She escaped and lived to tell the tale."

He felt a smile creep across his mouth. "Which begs the question, will you manage to do the same?"

Something flickered in her eyes. Despite the darkness, he could see her quite clearly. The moon was almost full and the sky clear and bright. The water around them reflected its platinum rays, painting them both with an eerie light that made the scene look like an old black-and-white photograph.

"Only time will tell."

His question spooked her, because she swung her shapely legs down to the floor and reached for her now-dry swimsuit. Lust sneaked up around the edges of his brain again as she pulled it on over her slim body. Then she wrapped a towel around herself and stood staring out over the water, where the first bright shimmers of dawn licked at the horizon. "Can we go back now?"

He suppressed the sigh that filled his chest. He'd have liked to stay out here for a week with her, with no one to disturb them and the outside world no more significant than a flashing message light on his phone. "If you insist, m'lady."

"I do." She shot him a smile. "A girl needs to powder her nose now and then, you know."

He chuckled at the idea of Vicki powdering her nose. Although who knows, maybe she did? He heaved himself up, grabbed his trunks and headed for the bridge, comforting himself with the thought that the cup—if it was ever there in the first place—must be very well hidden in the sand and coral rock and could take a good long time to find.

They slept in late in their shared perch under the fresco. Vicki awoke first and sat bolt upright as the memory of the last day and night flooded back into her sleep-refreshed brain. Okay, so they'd slept together. No biggie. Not like it was the first time or anything.

But damn was it beautiful.

She slid carefully off the bed so as not to wake him. A quick glance behind her revealed that he was as dangerously handsome as she remembered. Worse yet, his eyes were cracked open and he was watching her.

"Worried I'll try to make a run for it?"

"Nope." His mouth hitched into an arrogant smile that made irritation and desire shimmer through her. "Too far to swim."

"Go back to sleep. I want to be alone." She didn't look at him as she said it and she hoped she sounded stern. She did need some time to herself to process what was happening. There was nothing worse than getting swept along a tide of events and finding yourself washed up somewhere you never expected and couldn't get back from.

She'd showered before getting into bed, so she grabbed some panties and a sundress from her stash in the chest, along with her phone, and slipped out of the room.

Once out of their shared space, she allowed herself to lean against the wall and take a deep breath. What a night. Other men didn't make love to her like Jack. What was different? He held her with such passion and conviction. It was almost hard to believe that he didn't love her. Maybe he threw himself into everything like that?

She pried herself off the wall and wandered to the kitchen, where she helped herself to a glass of orange juice. The tart liquid puckered her tongue and made her shiver. Jack Drummond. Again. Had she really expected at any point that she could manage to avoid having sex with him? It came as no surprise that his boat was well stocked with a variety of condoms, not that she needed them. She didn't leave that kind of thing to chance and was already protected.

At least her womb was protected. Her heart, not so much.

Two friends had left messages on her phone, wondering where she was. She hadn't told anyone about her jaunt down to Florida. She hadn't wanted anyone to know what she was up to in case she chickened out. Or failed.

Seventeen missed calls, all from the same number. Leo Parker. Seventeen times he'd called and not left a message? Did he think she couldn't tell he was stalking her like some nut job from a horror movie? Except that he wasn't scary—more sad and lame. She was half-tempted to call him back and tell him exactly what she thought of him. But it didn't pay to make enemies, especially in her world, where everybody knew everybody. She'd tick him off, then find out that his aunt was a top curator at the Met.

Her ears pricked at the sound of feet padding down the corridor toward her. A puma on the prowl. She cursed her body's instant response to the nearing presence of Jack Drummond. How did he have that much power over her—again?

It's just lust. He's big and bold and male, and you've been deprived of sexual satisfaction for too long. Yeah, that was it. "Couldn't stay away, huh?" She challenged him with a hard stare as he entered the room.

It took tremendous effort to keep her eyes off his bare, bronzed chest, which was ridiculous as she'd had ample opportunity to grow bored with it on the boat yesterday. Maybe it was just her connoisseur's eye for well-formed *objets*.

"Nope." His confidence was adorable and infuriating at the same time. Jack Drummond never felt the need to sneak around or try to play it cool. He was simply... Jack. "And I thought I'd better make you breakfast. You don't look like you know how to cook."

"I hate cooking."

"I remember. That's why I'm going to make you waffles with papaya from my backyard."

Her stomach betrayed her with a fierce rumble. "Apparently my body says that would be fantastic."

His smile made her heart squeeze. Why did he have to be so nice? Arrogant, sure, obnoxious, too, but beneath the sun-scorched surface Jack Drummond was a straight-up nice guy.

Unless you needed to depend on him. She reminded herself that he valued his independence—his freedom—above all else, and anyone who forgot that for even an instant would learn the hard way, sooner or later.

But she wasn't going to make that mistake again.

They spent the day out on the boat and in the water digging around in the sand. Having determined that there was definitely a full ship there, and it would be a big project to unearth it, they decided to call for reinforcements. Jack phoned around to his crew, swearing them to secrecy. He grew silent after the last phone call.

"Dirk says he just got a call from Lou Aarons wanting him to dive for the same wreck." An uncharacteristic furrow had appeared in his tanned brow.

"Impossible. No one knows it's there."

"They didn't until now, but it's easy enough to spot when someone's up to something. We probably never even noticed one more helicopter in the air or another boat not far off while we were diving. People know my boat, so if it's anchored in one place for too long, they start to make assumptions."

Vicki chewed her lip. Could someone else really dig the cup right out from under them? In reckless moments she'd imagined she might ask for a cut of any gold coins or bullion they found, and now she was at risk of losing even the small reward she needed so badly. "Can we stake a claim to the site?"

"Sure, but it takes time. No one's going to come blow our boat out of the water, but they can start searching the same area. In wrecks, the debris scatters far enough that your cup fragment could be half a mile away. That's why the team will help. They know how to get the seabed up and poke around in there fast. We'll go ashore and get some supplies, then we can stay out on the water day and night until we find what we need."

Vicki wondered exactly what Jack needed. It wasn't the cup fragment, for sure. He was probably excited about finding his pirate ancestor's stolen goods. She had to admit that she was pretty excited about that, too. The prospect of fondling eighteenth-century emeralds almost took her mind off the intense sensations and emotions last night had awoken in her.

They headed to the local marina for refueling and Jack went into a boat repair shop to buy some parts. Vicki went into a small market and stocked up on basic food supplies and gallon jugs of water. She had just loaded them on the boat and disembarked to go find herself a cappuccino when she heard footsteps behind her on the wood planking of the quay.

"What a surprise." A male voice with a distinctive and highly recognizable sarcastic undertone. Leo Parker.

She spun around, out of alarm as much as recognition. "What are you doing here?"

"On vacay with my old mate Iago. Know him? He owns Viscaya Investments."

She shrugged. She'd heard of him, and none of it was good. "Oh." How could she get away from him? This time, if he asked her to dinner, she'd be sure to answer with a firm *no*.

"Didn't you get my messages?" His rather low forehead furrowed beneath his mop of coiffed blond hair.

She shook her head. "I lost my phone. Had to buy a new one." Hopefully her nose wasn't growing. If it was, she deserved it for stringing him along in the first place. Had he tracked her down here? Her gut clenched.

"Oh, that explains it." He smiled that annoying vacant smirk she'd sworn never to subject herself to again. "Iago's gone back to New York for a few days, so I have his house and boat to myself. I was thinking you could join me for some R & R."

She glanced around. No sign of Jack. Her gut was sending out all kinds of warning signals right now. What world of delusion did this guy live in? "I can't, I'm afraid. I'm here with a friend and we're really busy." Annoyingly she couldn't go into any detail as this idiot would be quite capable of telling everyone he knew and inadvertently or otherwise drawing the attention of every treasure hunter on the East Coast.

"I'm sure you can make a little time for me, Vicki." The way he said her name made a little shiver creep up her spine. His watery pale blue eyes fixed on her in a steely stare she didn't remember seeing before. "Because I know more about you than I've let on."

She froze. What could this jerk know about her? She'd been careful to reveal absolutely nothing about herself while eating expensive dinners with him. "I really have to go." She gestured back at the boat she'd just left. She didn't even want to tell him she was going into the deli for coffee or he might take it as an invitation. Where was Jack? The boat shop was way over on the far side of the marina, a big hangar of a building, and he was probably still inside it.

"I know about your dad's bankruptcy."

She swallowed. Her father had never declared bankruptcy. The complexity of his investments—or perhaps the illegality of some of them—made that impossible.

He'd simply gone broke. But to say anything at all would confirm what he apparently knew—her family was wiped out financially and so was she. "I don't know what you're talking about."

He laughed, an ugly stuttering sound. "Let's not play games, Vicki. You need money. I have money. We enjoy each other's company, and we have a lot in common." He held out one of his limp, pale hands. "Come out for a nice dinner with me and we'll talk over some plans."

She recoiled and a wave of panic rose through her. "I can't go out to dinner with you now or ever again. I'm engaged to marry someone else." She said it loud and firm. And it wasn't until the words had left her mouth that she noticed Jack, climbing out of a red-and-white boat only a few yards away.

Seven

Vicki didn't know where to look. She wanted to run fast and far. Had Jack heard her entire conversation with Leo? She'd rather die than have him know she was flat broke. He'd pity her, and that would be a fate worse than death.

He'd obviously heard the last part because he walked toward them, slid a proprietary arm around her waist and squeezed her. "Everything okay, angel?"

The odd, affectionate term made her blink. "Uh, yeah. I was just heading back to the boat." She supposed she should introduce Leo, but because Leo was obviously a nutcase, he might take that as a cue to invite himself to dinner at Jack's house. Being rude seemed more sensible.

"Jack Drummond." He thrust the arm that wasn't around her waist toward the shorter man. Apparently

Jack couldn't resist digging deeper. "Are you a friend of my fiancée?" He dug her ribs a little bit on the last word.

She felt color rising to her cheeks—and that didn't happen often.

"We are friends. I had no idea she was engaged." Leo looked flustered, probably wondering why she hadn't mentioned this before.

Jack's gaze scorched the side of her face. "It was a very sudden engagement. We don't even have our rings yet. We've loved each other for years, of course." Jack wasn't doing a good job of hiding the humor in his voice. "Vicki's come to live with me here on my houseboat."

If she weren't trying to prop up this pretense, she'd have slapped him and said she'd rather live in a tent in the Gobi than on a houseboat with him. Instead, she said, "I've always loved the water," and managed a simpering smile.

She could feel a chuckle of laughter rising in Jack's mighty chest, which was pressed against her side.

"Well, little lady, we'd better get back on the boat so you can rustle us up some dinner." He squeezed her again. She fought the urge to shove him off the dock into the water. "It was nice meeting you, Mr...."

Leo apparently realized he hadn't managed to introduce himself. "Parker. Leo Parker." His voice sounded a little shaky. This was not going at all according to plan for him, thank goodness. Jack was cheeky to insist on getting his name.

Hmm, maybe he was jealous?

That thought brightened her dark mood.

Leo Parker shrank away, and Vicki heaved a sigh of relief as Jack guided her back to the boat. Once safely on board, she turned to make sure Leo was nowhere around. She saw his dejected form climbing into a large black SUV in the marina parking lot. "Hey, I never got my coffee."

"That guy had no idea we were engaged." Jack turned to her, eyes sparkling with amusement. "Funny thing is, neither did I."

"That guy's a creep. I was trying to get rid of him." Did Jack overhear the part about her father going bust? She certainly wasn't going to ask. "I hope he didn't follow me down here."

"How could he know where to find you?"

She shrugged. "I did get my mail forwarded. And Katherine Drummond obviously figured out I was coming because she told you. You found me pretty easily." She glanced over. The SUV was still sitting in the parking lot. Maybe Leo Parker was in there, watching them on the boat deck. She shuddered. "Maybe he installed a tracking device on me last time I was foolish enough to accept his invitation to dinner."

Jack didn't look at all jealous. He was probably thinking she must be very lonely and desperate to date the likes of Leo Parker. He'd be right, of course, but she didn't want him to know that. "I suppose if he doesn't take a hint, I'll have to defend your virtue." He started the motor and looked amused by the prospect.

"Thanks for your support. He's staying with Iago Knoll, so he's not going anywhere just yet. Yuck." She shivered again.

"Why did you go out with him?"

"I didn't know he'd turn into a stalker."

"I suppose that is hard to predict." They pulled out of the marina. Jack's reassuring presence comforted her when she took a last glance at the marina—and saw that SUV was still there. "But he doesn't seem like your kind of guy."

"What exactly is my kind of guy?" She crossed her arms over her chest. Jack's infuriating arrogance was a nice distraction right now.

"Me, of course." She could only see him in profile, but she didn't miss his mouth curving upward slightly.

"Very sure of yourself, aren't you?"

"I suspect that's one of the things you find attractive about me." He didn't turn around to catch her expression. He didn't have to. No doubt he knew she'd be fuming, and thinking he was right.

"Don't get a big head. I'm only after your muscular body."

"And my world-renowned treasure hunting skills." She saw one eyebrow lift.

"Yeah, that, too. Are we going back to the site tonight?"

"Nope, first thing tomorrow we're picking the crew up here and heading out there as a group. You'll get to meet the guys."

"Great. Are you going to introduce me as your fiancée?"

His booming laugh gave her all the answer she needed.

In bed that night, she toyed with the prospect of rejecting him before he could reject her. Because the idea of their being engaged was so plainly laughable—and really, it was—then their relationship had an expiration date which was fast approaching. Someone was going to get dumped, and this time she was determined it wouldn't be her.

But when his big hand settled on her waist, a thick curl of lust unfolded low inside her, and her resolve faltered. Why should she deny herself the simple and healthy pleasure of having steamy-hot sex with the best lover she'd ever known? A sensible woman knew when to take advantage of what was on offer. Just because she relished sex with him didn't mean she was falling in love. She could enjoy the pleasures of the flesh, then walk away without a backward glance.

Right?

That night held a few dangerous moments, like after her third orgasm, when her mind began to play tricks, and fantasies of living happily ever after with Jack stalked the edges of her imagination. Then again when she let herself drift off to sleep in the safe embrace of his big, strong arms. For once she didn't feel as though she had to fight anyone or anything, or worry about what tomorrow would bring. Jack was in charge and he had it covered. His team of brawny experts would dive off the boat with their high-tech search equipment, and she could probably kick back with a virgin margarita and watch pelicans circle overhead. She'd be stuck on the boat, likely with no cell phone signal and no appointments or plans or rich people to suck up to. Which sounded ideal.

Right now she was Jack Drummond's willing prisoner—or was he hers? This whole thing was her idea anyway. Being marooned on Jack's boat was a welcome vacation from real life and she might as well make the most of it.

* * *

Jack's crew included four men ranging in age from early twenties to late fifties. All seemed excited and happy to be there. Jack gave her full credit for locating the wreck and treated her with the same demeanor as the rest of the crew. Which should make her feel relieved and happy. All she really cared about was finding that old piece of barnacle-encrusted cup and getting the heck out of here to claim the reward for it.

Right?

They headed out for the wreck site in two boats. When they got there, they anchored the smaller one and gathered on Jack's main boat to prepare for the dive. They were all on deck checking their equipment when Jack moved up behind her, slid his arms around her waist and kissed her cheek.

She gasped. All four of the men could simply lift their heads and watch. Embarrassment flashed over her, mingled with indignation. Was he showing off? Proving to them that he could have any woman he wanted with just the touch of his sturdy finger? Not one of them even glanced up. Maybe Jack always brought a broad along on treasure hunts for good luck, like the figureheads on old wooden boats.

She wanted to slap him away and mock him for being unable to keep his hands off her. To save face and show them all that she wasn't yet another pathetic woman drooling over the great Jack Drummond.

Instead, she found herself melting at the touch of his lips on her cheek, the warm circle of his hands around her waist. And when she kissed him back, her eyes slid closed and she forgot all about the men, and the sea and the sun and the sunken wreck and the missing cup and Leo Parker and all that other mess that cluttered up her brain. Nothing existed but her and Jack, locked in a passionate embrace and kissing each other as if it was the last thing they'd ever do.

He pulled back first, leaving her blinking and breathless in the sunlight. She stepped back too fast, trod on an oxygen tank and had to grab his arm to steady herself.

"You diving?" His brusque question ignored all that went before.

"Sure." Suddenly she didn't want to be the mascot sitting on the boat waiting for the menfolk to come back. "Let's get going." She tried to distract herself with checking her scuba gear and strapping it all on. Jack had moved to the other side of the boat and was going over some details of how to map out the wreck with one of the crew. Much better to be under the water keeping busy than sitting up here mooning over a man with a proven record of breaking her heart.

The dive lasted all day, with a raucous break for kebabs, which one of the guys had brought in a cooler and barbecued on a hibachi right on the deck. The whole crew was obviously stoked about the wreck.

Mel was the oldest, with years of commercial fishing experience before dipping his feet in the treasure hunting world. Silver-haired but with the tanned body of a young man, he found humor in everything. Jovial Greg regaled them with stories of a recent deep-sea fishing trip in the Bahamas with a famous music producer and his supermodel wife who thought fishing was murder. Luca was a handsome Italian with a rich accent and a flirtatious manner that might have been diverting if she wasn't already too sensually on edge for that kind of thing. And Ethan was an enthusiastic college kid who thought every piece of equipment and technique was the coolest thing ever. They all treated Jack with a reverence that would be impressive if it wasn't so annoying.

"Vicki's my lucky charm." Jack smiled at her through a bite of kebab during lunch. "I think the wreck was waiting for her arrival to reveal itself."

"Ships do have their feelings." Mel smiled at her. "Any old sailor will tell you that. And now she's rising up right into our hands to welcome us." They'd blasted away more of the sand to find the wreck in surprisingly intact condition. "Almost like the sleeping beauty's been lying under her blanket for three hundred years waiting for us to come wake her up."

"Vicki's most interested in one-third of a family chalice that went down with the wreck. At least we assume it did. It could be on a shelf behind the bar of a tavern in Kingston, Jamaica." Jack winked at her. "But even if we don't find that, we'll be rewarded for our work." He nodded toward the plastic bins already filling with items retrieved from the ship. Right now it looked like a bunch of unidentifiable rocks, all glued together with coral and who knew what else. But she'd heard them exclaim over coins and buckles and pieces of weaponry, so there were probably emerald rings and pearl combs and plenty of other treasures in there somewhere.

"Lucky we got out here so fast. Look who's over there." Greg nodded his head to the south where a large, white boat was clearly visible.

Mel chuckled and shook his head. "Lou Aarons. Always one step behind. I swear that guy just watches where Jack's boat goes and starts digging nearby."

"Let old Lou have our leftovers." Jack grinned and

took a swig of iced tea. "There's no need for us to be greedy when we have this kind of bounty at our fingertips. As long as he doesn't get Vicki's cup." He flashed a glance at her.

Her insides quivered like a subterranean jellyfish in a riptide. Already she couldn't stop thinking about tonight, and all the things he might do to her in the privacy of their shared bedroom. But she attempted to look calm and collected. "And don't forget that it probably doesn't look like a cup. It might be the base. So any unidentified metal objects you find, please show them to me even if they look totally useless."

They all agreed, and Mel told a story about a twisted old piece of encrusted metal he'd found that had turned out to be an ancient pre-Incan breastplate made out of nearly a pound of solid gold.

They dived all afternoon, and had filled ten large plastic tubs with "finds" before calling it a day just before sunset. Ethan was to sleep overnight on the boat and guard the site while the others returned to shore in the smaller boat. Jack and Vicki dropped the three remaining crew members off at the marina and headed back to the island, taking their booty with them.

Even though her body was tired from all the diving, Vicki's mind was crackling with excitement to examine the items that had been pried from the sea's grasp after nearly three hundred years of entombment. Even the prospect of getting naked with Jack paled in comparison to shining a bright light on the mysterious treasures in those plastic tubs.

"We need to keep them wet." Jack had half filled each container with salt water, making them unwieldy to unload from the boat. "We don't want them exposed to oxygen in the air until we know what we're dealing with."

"Aye-aye, Cap'n."

"I'm beginning to think you're part seal. You don't have any problem diving for hours along with the rest of us who do it all the time. And what happened to your seasickness?"

Vicki shrugged. "I have to admit I'm enjoying myself. Makes a big change from pounding the streets of Manhattan trying to make a deal over a Peretti brooch."

She pulled a concretelike lump with visible metal protrusions from one of the tubs. "How do you tell what anything is?"

"This big lump is called a concretion. We usually start with either a chisel or an X-ray machine, depending on how delicate and possibly valuable the items are. In this case I vote for the X-ray."

The X-ray machine was portable, and Jack set it up like a camera to focus on each object as they placed it on a taped X on a glass-topped table in his living room.

"Here X does really mark the spot." Vicki's stomach tingled with excitement as she placed the first heavy, wet concretion on the table. "What's the strangest thing you've ever found in a lump like this?"

Jack held the X-ray machine up and she moved well out of the way while he took the image. "A full set of solid gold teeth inside a skull."

"Eek! I shouldn't have asked. I guess that was pirate fashion back in the day."

"Probably held up better than the more popular wooden teeth." He put the X-ray machine down and scrutinized a monitor. "Hmm."

"What?" She moved around so she could see the

image. Several long, wavy shapes stood out against the textured background. She could see some curved masses, too.

"Could be knives. That looks like a mug. We might have found the kitchen."

"Could be a good place for part of an old chalice to be stored." She sneaked a glance at him.

"Yeah, as if it could be that easy." He chuckled. "There's definitely some interesting stuff in here, so this is when we get out the chisels. But we'll save that for later."

They ate baked ziti that his housekeeper had prepared and left for them to reheat, then they x-rayed several more concretions. One held some small round shapes that Jack recognized as coins, but he didn't seem excited enough to liberate them. Probably old coins weren't even thrilling to him anymore. A man only needed but so much treasure. There were plenty of shapes that looked as though they could be part of an old cup, which was either encouraging or quite the opposite, depending on how you looked at it.

As they neared midnight she found herself growing impatient for the next activity on her agenda—bedtime with Jack.

"I think we should get some sleep." Vicki's voice made Jack glance up from the monitor.

"Is it late?" He lost all track of the time when they made a new find. The adrenaline rush that accompanied discovering buried history could keep him awake for days.

"To most people, yes." She didn't look tired. She did look gorgeous. "I'm going to hit the sack."

"Okay." He adjusted the brightness on the monitor. Something in there was quite unusual. Delicate and multifaceted—like a piece of jewelry, perhaps. Too early to tell, but still... Maybe he could take the time to chisel delicately at this one.

"Aren't you coming?" Vicki hovered in the doorway. She was dressed in a long, thin T-shirt—and some tempting black underwear he'd noticed when she bent over to pick up the concretions—and looked very inviting.

"In a while." The mysterious object tugged his attention back to the monitor. Gold had a certain quality to it in an X-ray image. At least it did to him. Smoother, lighter than silver. He could spot it almost by instinct.

"I might get lonely." Her soft words jerked his head up from the screen. Vicki had summoned him to bed. This was new. Up until now he'd been doing all the flirting and chasing—which had been so worth it—and expecting only prickly reluctance in return.

Apparently now it was his turn to be seduced. "In that case, I'd better come with you." He switched off the equipment and followed her down the hallway. Her slim hips had a seductive swing to them that set his blood pumping. Even eighteenth-century gold paled in comparison to the swaying body of a beautiful woman beating a path to his bedroom.

And what a woman. He'd been keeping an eye on her diving equipment himself, to make sure she was doing everything right, but his caution had been unnecessary. Vicki could take care of herself. She'd fit in perfectly with the guys, and dived like a professional, with no complaints and an enthusiasm that rivaled his own.

In addition to being beautiful, she was smart and

sharp and funny. He even enjoyed her frosty barbs and cutting glances. In fact, he liked them better than the simpering and mewing of the more typical girls who crowded around him in bars begging for tales of treasure.

Vicki, Vicki, Vicki.

He followed her into the bedroom, and paused to savor the view as she pulled her T-shirt off over her head. The black panties were scanty, with a design that revealed more than it covered. If they were designed to deprive men of their powers of speech, then they worked like a charm.

She climbed up on the high bed—a move that sent blood rushing to his groin—and lay there, eyes half-closed in a seductive expression.

He ripped off his jeans and T-shirt and strode across the room, excitement percolating in his veins. He kissed her lips softly, then rougher, taking the kiss deeper until that first sweet moan of pleasure escaped them.

He teased her body with his mouth, feathering kisses over her breasts and belly, then licking her sex until it pulsed with anticipation. His own arousal was almost unbearable. Vicki's long, elegant fingers plucked at the skin of his back and roamed through his hair with abandon, while her sighs filled the air like music.

His level of arousal could probably be measured in degrees Fahrenheit by the time he finally let himself enter her. She was so eager, gripping him and tugging him closer, pawing him and kissing him, her eyes closed tight.

When he filled her, she said his name over and over, as if trying to convince herself it was really him. He needed no convincing that he was with Vicki St. Cyr, the most compelling and confusing and original and wonderful woman he'd ever had the pleasure to know. Part of him despised his weakness in being afraid of her power and passion all those years ago. She was a force of nature, like a tornado that sucked up everything in its path.

At least back then she was. Now she was quieter, cooler, more subtle. But perhaps no less forceful, like a riptide hidden beneath the surface, silent and invisible until the unwitting swimmer has been sucked halfway to the horizon.

These thoughts rolled in his mind as their bodies rolled on the bed. He'd been afraid of her then, although he'd rather have died than admit it. She was so sure of herself, so aware of her power over men and everyone else. Her confidence—her arrogance—had been a core part of her charm. No one dared to argue with her because they knew they'd lose. Playing with Vicki was like playing with a baby tiger or an open flame—you never knew quite when it would turn on you and leave you hurting.

So he'd done the cowardly thing and saved himself by running away.

He'd tried to lose himself in the soft embraces of other women. Tried to distract himself with work and travel and new exciting projects. For a long time he thought he was over her. Then he'd heard she was coming to town and got so impatient to see her that he tracked her down to the hotel. She'd swept back into his life like a sirocco, turned it upside down and reminded him of why he'd been so wary of her in the first place.

Why did she come back? Her excuse of finding the

cup and claiming the reward only made sense if she was desperate for money. Which was hard to imagine.

Vicki's tongue shot into his ear and he gasped with raw sensation, driving deeper inside her and rolling again until she was on top. If a quest for cash brought Vicki back into his life, it certainly hadn't brought her back into his bed. She was every bit as hot and hungry for him as he was for her, and not shy about showing it, either.

When he shifted back on top, he kissed her face through the damp tendrils of her hair, drinking in her heady feminine scent. This woman drove him crazy in the best possible way. He increased the pace until he felt her climax take her by storm, and finally let go of all the agonizing but pleasurable tension building inside him.

They drifted back to the soft pillows together, chests heaving and skin moist with perspiration. Having Vicki in his bed felt so right. He opened his eyes to see the bright fresco she'd revealed. He'd slept under it for years with no idea it was there, just like he'd been sleepwalking through life without her.

Was Vicki back for a reason more profound than simply finding an object? Maybe she'd come back into his life as a sign that it was time for him to…

The words *settle down* crossed his consciousness and made him shift uncomfortably on the mattress. Then he wanted to laugh. Life with Vicki St. Cyr would be anything but settled. She was as restless and easily bored as himself, always chasing new pleasures and mysteries.

Life with Vicki St. Cyr…

Was that the life he was meant to live? The question rang in his heart and he found himself letting it vibrate there. Did she feel the same way? Her feelings were hard to determine as she was secretive and wily by nature.

Her eyes were closed, long dark lashes resting against her soft clear skin. Then she opened them and pierced him with that relentless violet gaze.

Did she know what he was thinking?

Her thoughts were a mystery to him as always. He wasn't usually inclined to look beneath the surface of things unless there was treasure there. But Vicki intrigued him and he wanted to plumb her secrets depths and enjoy her hidden facets.

Then her eyes closed again. She was tired after their long day. A protective instinct filled his chest. He needed to make sure she got a good night's sleep and didn't exhaust herself. She'd been pale and gaunt when she arrived, and sun and sea air and good food—and the invigorating sex, of course—were already working magic on her, but he'd better make sure she didn't overdo it.

Vicki shifted slightly, and blew out a soft breath. She seemed so relaxed now, all her defenses down. A smile played across her delicate features, and he could see her eyes moving beneath her eyelids, so she must be dreaming.

Was she dreaming about him? He hoped so because the dream looked like a good one. A tiny chuckle rose in her throat and she leaned toward him—still fast asleep—until their noses were almost touching.

She opened her pretty, dark pink mouth and another soft sigh brushed his skin. Then she murmured something, very quietly, like it was a secret. No one was meant to hear it.

But he did, and her words caused his blood to still in his veins.

Eight

Vicki woke suddenly, disoriented by the bright sunlight. A quick glance at the bed revealed that Jack was gone. What time was it? She climbed off the bed and checked her phone. How could it be 9:20? They were supposed to head back to the wreck at first light.

Slipping a T-shirt over her nakedness, she opened the bedroom door and peered down the sunlit corridor. "Jack?"

"Good morning, senorita." A short, dark-haired woman shot out of the room right next to her, making her jump. Jack's housekeeper. "You must be Vicki."

"And you must be Paloma. Jack's always talking about you." After watching Jack's cousin Sinclair fall madly in love with his own housekeeper, she had to admit relief that Jack's was old enough to be his mother.

Uh-oh. Did this mean she was jealous?

"It would be funny if I wasn't Vicki, wouldn't it?" She wished she had more than a T-shirt on. It was painfully obvious what she and Jack had been up to last night. Paloma had probably witnessed a lot of morning-after scenes and she hated being a stereotype.

She wanted to ask if Jack had left on the boat, but didn't want to admit that she didn't already know the answer.

"Jack told me to let you sleep in. He said you worked too long and hard yesterday." Paloma took on a bossy tone that was strangely reassuring. "He also told me to make you a huge breakfast, then let you do whatever you like with all the rocks and stuff in the living room." She shook her head. "Why he can't do that in the workshop, I don't know. Seawater isn't good for wood floors."

"No, I don't suppose it is." So Jack had left her alone with the treasure. She could spend her day whittling pirates' toothpicks out of the hunks of coral rock. Normally that would pass for a pretty interesting day, but somehow she felt hurt that Jack had abandoned her here. Maybe this was a subtle message that the team moved faster and more efficiently without her.

Or maybe this was the beginning of the big brush-off.

"Do you have grapefruit?"

"Of course we do." Paloma smiled. "And I baked fresh biscuits. How about I scramble some eggs to go with them?"

"Sounds heavenly." Her stomach growled in agreement. So what if Jack wasn't here. She could use a break from overexposure to his tanned and brawny physique. And an afternoon nap might be a welcome luxury, as well.

After breakfast she wandered outside to look for the ship in the distance. She couldn't see it, though, so it must be just over the horizon. The day was warm, with sensual, languid weather, perfect for relaxing in a hammock. But she couldn't resist being the first person to handle items that had gone down with the wreck, for the first time in hundreds of years.

She booted up the computer they'd used the night before and found the files of the X-rays, then printed them all out. Although the missing cup piece didn't seem all that riveting when compared to the prospect of looted Spanish gold and stolen jewelry, she figured she should at least scan the images for anything promising.

On the third image something caught her eye. A delicate filigree of metal entwined deep in the concretion of sand and coral. Her heart pounded as she scrutinized the shape and made out what looked like the outline of a large and elaborate necklace with the chain still attached.

She located the big chunk of seabed labeled with the same number as the image, and the tray of chisels Jack had shown her. She kept the rock in its plastic container, marinating in a few inches of seawater. No need to risk it crumbling to dust, and it would probably make less mess to keep the water contained. As Paloma vacuumed somewhere in the distance, she took a medium chisel to the lump of sandy rock.

The crust was surprisingly hard, and when it broke it tended to shatter into large chunks. She switched to a smaller chisel for more precision. The last thing she wanted was for Jack to return home and find she'd dented or broken a priceless antique. Eventually, she found a rhythm and refined her technique, and sometime around noon, the long-lost piece started to emerge from its stony tomb.

She saw a chain-link first, and immediately switched to the finest chisel on the tray, removing the sandy accretion almost grain by grain.

Gold. The chain was unmistakably made from its era's most precious metal. Untarnished by its long burial, it gleamed in the reflected sunlight shining through the window as if it had been waiting all this time to show itself.

Quite thick, the links were bent and twisted but all intact. The pendant attached to the chain was also gold, dented and squarish in shape, and looked as if something was missing. It had no gems. Possibly Jack's coarse ancestors had pried them off and traded them in a game of dice.

She laughed. She should be mad that Jack had ditched her, but she couldn't be. This was too much fun.

After Paloma left for the day, she indulged in that nap she'd fantasized about. She swung gently from a hammock strung beneath two palm trees on the lawn in the shade of the ubiquitous sea grape. Her dream drew her into a sensual realm not unlike last night's antics in bed. Apparently her brain and body couldn't get enough of Jack so they had to conjure him even when he wasn't here.

Disturbing. And it did not bode well for her easily forgetting him when this affair was over.

Jack returned shortly after dark. She'd rummaged around in the kitchen and found a casserole Paloma must have started in the slow cooker. She set the table and poured two glasses of wine, then lit the candles above the fireplace and took time to fix her face and hair so he'd be pleasantly surprised to see her rather than annoyed she was still underfoot.

He walked into the foyer and smiled as soon as he saw her. "We missed you." His words touched her. So did the rough hug he gave her. His T-shirt was damp with sea spray. His skin smelled delicious and she had to fight the urge to lick him.

"I missed you, too. Just a little. But I kept busy."

"I'll bet you did. Find anything good?"

"Of course. I've piled the stash on that funky dresser in the living room." It seemed entirely appropriate for pirate treasure to be strewn here and there about an eclectic house, rather than catalogued and stored in plastic containers in a lab. Although, being fully aware of the crucial importance of a detailed provenance for each piece, she'd taken pictures at every stage of her chiseling and labeled each item with a catalog number. The Smithsonian would be proud of her. "I found a necklace, four musket balls, a fork, two rings and a jug. And that was all in one lump o' stone."

"Impressive." He grinned and held her closer. His hands cupped her backside, and he laid another kiss on her cheek.

A smile sneaked across her mouth. "I bet you didn't find as much stuff without me there for luck."

"You must have been there with us in spirit because we found a mother lode. Probably the cabin where the women sheltered from the storm."

"There were women on a pirate ship?"

He shrugged. "If you were a strapping, testosterone-fueled brigand, wouldn't you want a few ladies with you on your voyage?"

"Maybe one." She lifted an eyebrow. "Do you prefer a ménage?"

"No way." He kissed her other cheek. "I'm a one-
woman man."

One woman at a time, but not for long. She tried not
to let her thoughts show on her face. "Well, that's a relief. I got dinner ready, although I can't take any credit
for cooking. Paloma seems like a good woman to have
on your pirate ship."

"She's my secret weapon."

"How does she get here?"

"I have an old sea-dog friend ferry her out here from
the marina at nine every morning and take her back
at one."

"I'm glad to know that. I was beginning to think
there was magic involved. She made a casserole." She
gestured toward the dining room as casually as she
could. "I was about to dollop it into bowls and sling it
on the table." She tried to make her hospitality sound as
inhospitable as possible. She didn't want Jack to think
she was going soft in her old age.

Jack paused in the doorway when he saw the lit candles and sparkling glasses of wine. "Quite the elegant
repast to come home to."

Maybe you'll miss me when I'm gone. The thought
stayed in her mind. It was a foolish one because he
could just as easily get Paloma to set the table for him.
If he wanted a housewife, she was the last person in the
world she'd recommend for the job.

Would he miss her? She wondered if he'd missed her
the first time. Did you miss someone if you were
the one who left? Probably not. Your ears would still

be ringing with all the reasons you couldn't wait to get away from them.

She served out the casserole—it had a delicious wine scent—and sat down. Jack raised his glass. "To sharing my table with a woman who'd be the envy of my ancestors."

"They're all around us, aren't they?" She glanced about the large room with its high ceilings. If this were a more typical stately home, there would be large oil portraits decorating the walls. The plaster walls of Jack's dining room were hung with ornamental cutlasses and the fireplace mantel bore a decorative pyramid of pitted cannon balls.

Jack shrugged. "If they were, wouldn't they have told me where to find the wreck?"

"Maybe they're more entertained by watching you search for it. Did you find any bodies?"

"Nothing. Just the artifacts that would have been on them." He took a draft of white wine. "Sometimes the bodies disappear without a trace, which I much prefer."

She shivered. "Those poor people. I wonder if the ship went down fast."

"It must have if there was only one survivor. It's pretty close to shore so unless Lazaro Drummond dispatched everyone else with his salvaged musket, there should have been more people who made it back. I don't suppose we'll ever know what really happened. As you've observed, pirates don't keep the best records."

"They want to hold on to their mysteries." She could relate to that. It seemed that the longer she stayed here, the more of herself she revealed to Jack. And that wasn't good. "So you think much of the treasure was in that room?"

He nodded. "Looks that way. It's not unusual for seamen to put all their most valuable possessions in one locked room when a ship gets into trouble and they batten down the hatches. Then they know where it is and can retrieve it quickly if the ship starts to break up."

"And surely they'd have kept it under lock and key during the voyage anyway. I can't imagine a pirate trusting his own crew too far."

He lifted a brow. "You're wrong about that. If a pirate didn't trust a crew member he'd kill them as soon as look at them. You couldn't go out raiding ships if you didn't trust every last man—or woman—to defend your life with his own."

"So there was honor among thieves."

"Most of the time. The rest of them ended up in Dead Men's Cove."

After dinner she showed him her find and was pleased that he seemed impressed with her extraction techniques. He brought in the new tubs of findings, and they x-rayed them. There was an abundance of good stuff buried in the sandy lumps of stone.

"What if there are parts of several old chalices?" She stared at a black-and-white image on the monitor. "There might be such a thing as too much treasure."

"Then you take them all up to old cousin Sinclair's place and see if they fit together with the one he has there. How did they take the chalice apart?"

"From the look of the stem I'd guess the pieces just slid into each other with a tight fit. It certainly didn't screw in or anything crude like that. The stem part had smooth ends. We thought it would be pewter, but it turned out to be brass. The stem had some engraved decoration on it, so I'd imagine you could find similar decoration on the other parts and line up the pattern."

"A puzzle."

"Exactly."

"And if you solve it, I and the other Drummond heirs can live happily ever after."

"Or have a slightly better shot at happily ever after than you do now." It was hard to imagine Jack in some off-into-the-sunset ending where he lived peacefully with one woman for the rest of his life. He'd be bored stiff within a year. At least this time she wasn't going to be the woman he grew tired of. She'd leave fast enough to guarantee that.

In the meantime, could it really hurt to enjoy a little more hot sex?

Jack switched off the monitor. "We should get some sleep."

"I agree." Her skin tingled with the prospect of pressing itself against his. He looked very tempting right now in dark cotton pants and a faded logo T-shirt, but he'd look even more irresistible after she peeled them off.

"You sleep in my bed. I'll go next door."

"What do you mean next door?" Shock propelled the words from her mouth. Was there some hot next-door neighbor he was in the habit of visiting for a nightcap?

"The bedroom next door." He turned his back to her and strolled for the door like the decision had already been made. "Then we won't get distracted by… you know."

I sure do. And I was looking forward to the distraction. "I'm not that tired."

"You will be if you don't get some decent REM sleep. Don't you want to come out on the boat tomorrow?"

"I do, but I'm used to an active nightlife." If only he'd turn around she'd have a chance of charming him, but he kept moving farther down the corridor. She hurried to keep up. Then realized what she was doing.

He was already walking away from her. And she was chasing him like a lost puppy. "Actually a night of peace sounds really good." Let him sleep alone if he wanted to. She lifted her chin. She didn't need him. She just needed his treasure hunting expertise. And frankly they'd already had plenty of sex.

Her body argued with her, especially the parts that were already pulsing and tingling in eager anticipation of intimate union with Jack. She told it to be quiet. "See you in the morning." She hesitated. "You will wake me up tomorrow?" It sounded pathetic, like a dog putting the leash in its mouth and coming to its master. Still, she would be hurt to be left behind again.

Which was a problem. How did her emotional health suddenly depend on Jack Drummond's whims and fancies?

"Sure, I'll wake you. It'll be early."

She'd hoped for a good-night kiss at the very least, but he disappeared behind the carved wooden door next to his own bedroom, and she was left in the hallway, alone.

She blew out a breath. What had happened? Last night he was totally hot for her. They'd had the most intense and pleasurable sex she'd ever enjoyed in her life. Then in the morning he'd sneaked off without her. And now…

Something had happened.

But what?

* * *

Jack woke Vicki for breakfast with a gruff "Time to get going." He didn't want to go into the room and see her gorgeous body wrapped in a sheet. Better to get out on the boat with the boys where he'd have other things to keep his mind off her charms.

Tonight they'd put some serious effort into unpacking those concretions and maybe the cup would be in there. With that in her suitcase she could be back on her way again.

And right now, that seemed like the best thing that could happen.

He heard her shower running and imagined warm water cascading over those long, slim legs that displayed such athleticism in moments of passion. Then he distracted himself by measuring coffee into the filter. The world was full of beautiful women. Vicki was just one of them.

And she was one he did not intend to hurt any more than he already had.

Her words still vibrated in his ears, sending shards of guilt through him. *I've always loved you, Jack. Always.*

His stomach contracted at the memory. How could history repeat itself like that? Worse yet, he'd been toying with the possibility that Vicki St. Cyr might actually be "the one." Lord knows he couldn't imagine growing bored with her. She seemed to fit right in with his life here and she even brought finely honed analytical skills. And there was that strange, hollow feeling in his chest when he thought about her leaving.

Then she'd talked in her sleep and all those wayward thoughts had reeled back and snapped shut like an automatic tape measure. He wasn't ready for the responsibility of someone depending on him for their happiness.

I've always loved you. What the heck did that mean? Had she been pining for him all through the past six years? What kind of a nightmare was that? He'd thought of her from time to time, sure, but mostly he'd kept himself busy swimming with all the other lovely fish in the sea. And there were a lot of fish out there he hadn't swum with yet.

Cad.

His mom would tease him. She thought it funny that his reputation as a ladies' man was so well deserved. Because his notoriety followed him around like a flock of gulls after a fishing trawler, women generally knew what they were getting into when they climbed into his bed. With his roving lifestyle he didn't have to make excuses for why he couldn't come over for pot roast on Sunday. Everything was easy, casual.

"Morning." Vicki drifted into the room, her long silky black hair tousled. She wore a navy blue bikini under a sheer white T-shirt with the word *DARE* written on it in black.

His gut tightened. She wanted him to want her. And he did. That was the worst part. How could you turn down something so delicious right in front of you?

But Vicki was no longer some kid he could chalk up to life experience. She was a mature and experienced woman who'd come back to his house and into his bed. She put up a tough front, sure, but if what she said was true, then she'd been carrying a torch for him for years and he'd just poured kerosene on it.

"Orange juice?" He tried to sound casual. Like he

wasn't deliberating about the history of their relationship in his head.

"I prefer pomegranate." She cocked her head, still confident and challenging.

"You would." A grin tugged at his mouth. Damn, he was going to miss her. "How about coffee instead?"

"That'll do the trick."

He made French toast for both of them, and sliced some papaya. She kept the chatter going with questions about how the concretions form around the debris of the wreck, and he explained how it helped treasure hunters out immensely by keeping all the pieces more or less in one place over the centuries.

Damn, she was beautiful. It wasn't just her violet eyes or her smooth skin or the raven's wing hair, it was her whole demeanor—deadly cool and fiercely passionate at the same time. He'd never met anyone like her.

What if he never did again?

Vicki was glad to get out on the boat and keep busy tinkering with all the equipment and chatting with the guys. It took her mind off Jack's sudden change of heart toward her. The other men all sneaked sideways glances at her and hung on to her every word—which she was used to. Jack, on the other hand, seemed busy poring over charts he'd printed out and typing notes into a computer.

She tried not to let it hurt.

Of course it was embarrassing that Jack had kissed her in front of everyone on the first day out on the boat. There was no way she could pretend she'd kept him at a cool arm's length. Maybe they were all wondering why he was suddenly so distant and preoccupied.

She found herself itching to don her scuba gear and head down into the quiet world of the ocean where there was no room for conversation or sideways glances or speculating about someone's body language.

Jack's muscled body was a constant torment, tanned and toned and right in front of her at every moment. That she no longer had license to touch it only made it more tempting and distracting.

"Vicki, don't forget to check your tanks. I meant to do it but I haven't had a chance." He glanced over at her, pinning her with his hot gaze.

"Thanks for reminding me." She noticed with chagrin that one tank was almost empty. So much for her being self-reliant and not needing him. "There are so many things to keep track of when you're diving."

"It all takes practice. You're pretty on top of things for a landlubber."

It hurt to hear him call her that. Which was ridiculous. Since when did she want him to consider her an old salt? She meticulously checked the rest of her gear and looked around for anything else on the boat that might need fixing. She didn't want his team to think she was a fifth wheel.

Even if she was.

"Vicki, do you realize what you've done?"

She glanced up in shock when the youngest team member spoke.

"What?" She glanced down at her scuba gear, wondering what else she'd screwed up.

"You've found what's probably the most well-preserved eighteenth-century wreck in the history of the area." He shook his head, sun-bleached hair tossing in the wind. "I don't know how, but the word is getting out and the vultures are circling. Look." He pointed at a helicopter in the sky. She hadn't noticed it before, being used to them in New York, but as she watched, it circled them in a lazy loop. "The TV reporters will be next. They love a good treasure hunt. It boosts the ratings."

"Is that good or bad?"

"Good if you're trying to raise high prices for the artifacts. Bad if you're still trying to extract them. Worst-case scenario—someone can try to shut you down by citing some ancient claim to the treasure."

"How could they do that when the original owners are long dead and gone?"

"Sometimes the crown of a country will claim the spoils. Spain and Portugal have both laid claim to lost ships from their treasure fleets, never mind that the ships went down five hundred years earlier."

"Do they ever win?"

"They do."

"That's crazy." She squinted at Jack. "But this ship belonged to Jack's ancestor, which makes things a bit more cut and dried."

"Except that Jack's ancestor was a known pirate. If someone could prove a right to the stolen goods..." He shrugged. "You never know what people will do when there's gold involved."

Vicki felt a little surge of righteous indignation as she glanced up at the helicopter, still drifting overhead in wide circles. It was white and blue, obviously private, with no markings other than the number printed on the fuselage. Someone was spying on them.

With her luck, it was probably Leo Parker. She wondered if he'd spread the word about her whirlwind "engagement" to Jack and if she'd return to New York and have to unravel a lot of complicated rumors about her love life.

Her stomach clenched at the prospect.

"Let's dive!" With his usual enthusiasm, Jack led the charge over the side of the ship. She donned her mask and followed. The warm water closed over her head, shutting out the noise of the helicopter and dimming the bright sunlight to a muted glow.

She dived, kicking with her flippers to propel herself down into the cool, shadowy depths. At least down here no one could tell that she was already nursing the festering beginnings of a broken heart.

Nine

"Vicki should go on air." The team sat around Jack's ancient oak dining table. They'd returned the previous evening to a long string of phone messages from various local and international media outlets, all wanting the scoop on their discovery.

And they'd spent another night in separate beds. Jack's rejection of her—coming so much sooner than anticipated—hurt so much that she was almost numb.

And very, very sexually frustrated.

Yet she still had to put on a brave face and act as though everything was just fine. "No, really, I hardly know anything about the history of the vessel or the methods you're all using. It would be much better if someone else did the talking."

"I'll speak, of course." Jack frowned at the collage of maps he'd printed from his computer. She couldn't read them at all. A jumble of numbers that made less sense than the crazy Roman numeral code she'd unraveled. "And I agree that Vicki should go on camera. She solved a puzzle that's had the Drummonds stumped for centuries."

Something in her gut told her that going on air was not a good idea. What if some bright-eyed reporter started digging around in her past and found out about her father's financial problems? It was almost a miracle that that had never hit the press in the first place. "If you tell them about the treasure map, they'll want to come to the house and take pictures. Probably better just to say you were digging around and stumbled across it."

"No way!" Ethan protested. "The treasure map is the best part of the story. I can already see the Hollywood movie version with Russell Crowe as Jack and Demi Moore as Vicki. It's a great story."

"Demi Moore?" Vicki had to protest. "She's more than twenty years older than me!"

"And still damn hot." Jack grinned. "Maybe I'll ask them if I can play myself opposite her."

"You go ahead." She lifted her chin. "And if you want reporters traipsing all over your private island, then you might as well invite them."

Jack frowned. "Hmm, that does go against a deep-rooted Drummond instinct for privacy. On the other hand, unlike my ancestors, I don't really have anything to hide."

"Your island might become a tourist destination." She lifted a brow. "They'll bring boatloads of eager vacationers out here to see the famous Drummond lair."

"And I can start a sideline selling T-shirts and fake scrimshaw." Jack leaned back in his chair and wove his fingers behind this head, giving her yet another infuriating view of his tanned and bulging biceps.

Her insides throbbed and pulsed with frustrated lust. It was beyond cruel of him to lead her on and tantalize her with the hottest sex of her life, then leave her high and dry like this. There should be a law against that kind of cold-hearted torture. "And mugs with your sunburned face on them."

"Hey, I like it." His grin widened. "Then the big question is, who do we call first?"

Vicki wanted to sigh and hold her head in her hands. Instead, she kept a poker face. "How about you start with the most local outfit and let the story grow from there." Then hopefully she'd be long gone before the coverage got out of control. If she didn't find that cup by the end of this week, she'd be leaving without it. They'd brought up so much stuff already that if it wasn't in one of the plastic boxes piled high around the house and workshop, it was probably gone forever.

And with everything else that was happening she didn't really care much anymore. There had to be easier ways to earn ten thousand dollars. It was a shame that she'd decided she was too proud to ask Jack for a finder's fee or a cut of the treasure.

"All right, we'll go with WGX. I went deep-sea fishing once with the head of the news department and he seems like a stand-up guy."

"Perfect." She rose from her chair. Of course he'd go with some old sailor-boy network connection. She couldn't wait to get back to her own world where at least she had some connections of her own. "If you'll all excuse me, I'm going to go chisel out some more treasure."

* * *

Jack felt like a jerk. Vicki was hurt. And why wouldn't she be? She'd finally let down her guard and fallen into his beckoning arms only to have him push her away.

After he'd enjoyed some downright legendary good times with her.

If only she hadn't said that stuff about always loving him. His chest clenched just thinking about it.

Luckily he didn't have much time to dwell on his own shortcomings because the crew from WGX had already descended and was trailing wires around his living room and setting up white-hot lights everywhere. Vicki had sequestered herself in the workshop. Even though she'd insisted that she shouldn't appear on camera, he took note of her rather glamorous outfit and carefully made-up face and suspected she would be hurt if he didn't shove her in front of the reporters.

So he certainly didn't intend to fail in that regard. Damn, she looked gorgeous. Her white blouse was translucent enough to make a man sweat. Dark jeans hugged her sinfully long legs, emphasized by high-heeled sandals. The more primitive parts of his brain—or maybe it wasn't his brain at all—urged him to wrap his arms around her and bury his face in her scented black tresses.

"Hey, Jack, is it okay if they shoot some footage of your boat?" The door had opened and an eager female reporter peered in.

"Uh, sure." He tried to snap his attention back to the chaos unfolding in his personal sanctuary. Two more young women entered the room and stared at the boxes of artifacts.

"Is this the stuff from the ship?" The one with long red hair lifted one of the plastic lids.

"Yes." Vicki hurried over and closed the lid. "And it can't be exposed to air because of oxidization." She gave the girl a stern look.

Jack wanted to chuckle. Vicki as schoolmarm—now he'd seen everything. He bet she'd be a strict mother who made sure her kids had impeccable manners, then she'd let them stay up and scare themselves watching a late-night movie.

"Jack, why don't you explain oxidization to these young ladies?"

His gaze snapped to them and he realized with a chill that he'd been thinking about Vicki's maternal qualities. Obviously he was losing his mind. Vicki had boldly declared that she didn't want children, and he had no reason whatsoever not to believe her. Not that it mattered. He and Vicki were far too volatile a compound to share space for long, let alone to reproduce.

At least that's what his brain kept telling him. His gut was singing a different song. "What do you need to know about it?" He looked from one girl to the other. They looked like college students and were probably interns. Maybe Vicki was dangling them in front of him like minnows to see if he'd take a nibble.

"How does water prevent oxidization from occurring?"

"It forms a seal around the objects as long as they're immersed."

"But water is part oxygen," the earnest blonde with the ponytail protested.

"I know, but that doesn't seem to matter." He shrugged. "I'm not a chemist, just a treasure hunter.

Whatever works, I do it, and I don't worry too much about the hows and whys." He smiled.

They nodded and one of them lifted another lid. "So we can look at these objects as long as we don't lift them out of the water?"

Vicki shot Jack a stern look. "Only if it's okay with Vicki."

"I think it would be better if we selected a few objects and concretions for you to videotape." Vicki sounded businesslike, which was quite a contrast with her rock-star attire. "This container here has the visible remains of an old cannon ball embedded in the coral, and several pieces of a glass bottle. Why don't you help me carry it into the other room?"

He watched her leave with the two girls. It had half killed him not to sleep with her last night. And the night before. It seemed such a cruel waste of a beautiful opportunity. He knew he'd never get another chance to share a bed with Vicki St. Cyr.

Not unless he intended to take up a permanent berth there.

Once again the wild and unreasonable prospect of a real relationship with Vicki assaulted his brain like strong drink. No part of the idea made any sense. Yes, they had more chemistry than the Scripps Institute and the sex was transcendental, but beyond that, they had almost nothing in common. She loved the New York social scene, going to parties, making deals, and he liked nothing more than to be out on his boat in the middle of the ocean where no one could find him.

But to be out in the ocean with Vicki…

That was a fantasy come true, and that there was

treasure involved, as well? He should pinch himself because he must be dreaming.

The door swung open again. "We're ready to roll tape."

"Coming." He wandered back into the living room. As he'd expected, Vicki had already taken center stage and turned on her familiar blitzkrieg of charm. She laughingly agreed to share the story of the treasure map and show it to them. He found himself watching with pleasure. Vicki was like an old-time movie star—Lauren Bacall, maybe, or Audrey Hepburn. You could stare at her all day and never get bored. At least he could.

How would he feel when she was gone for good?

As the crew dragged cameras and lights into Jack's bedroom, Vicki found herself regretting her rash promise to show them the map.

"So, uh, how did you come to see the map in the first place?" The smiling female reporter gestured to the ceiling above the bed. Her lacquered cap of blond hair didn't move when she tilted her head.

Vicki cleared her throat. "Jack explained that his ancestor Lazaro Drummond had painted the map there to hide it from anyone but his intimate companions."

"Are we to infer that you and Jack are intimate companions?" She was joking—sort of—but Vicki felt her cheeks heat.

"Jack and I are old friends. Very old friends, but that's all." The lie reeled effortlessly off her tongue. Was it perjury to lie on the local evening news? It must be some kind of crime. She hoped Leo Parker wouldn't see this. It rather undermined her other lie about being engaged to Jack. She could feel Jack's gaze on her from the far side of the room, and she wondered what he was thinking. He was probably relieved. He obviously regretted their "intimacy" or he wouldn't be sleeping alone in a different bedroom.

"Jack, could you join us over here?" The reporter looked up from the clip-on mic she was adjusting and turned to where he leaned against the wall on the far side of the room. "I think it would be fun if you both told us the story."

Vicki stiffened. Being close to Jack made her circuits go haywire. Too much loose electricity buzzing in the air. He ambled across the room, looking uncharacteristically awkward.

The reporter, an elegant woman in her early thirties, simpered at him. "Perfect! All right. I think we're ready to roll tape." There was some bustling around and a director appeared. No one actually said "action," but suddenly it was happening. "Jack and Vicki, you discovered the mural together?"

"Vicki gets all the credit." Jack's voice sounded gruffer and deeper than usual. He was so close that the hairs on her arm stood on end, as if reaching out to touch his arm. "She was lying in bed and she noticed pits in the fresco that were a different color."

Vicki swallowed. Did he have to mention that she was lying in bed? Why not say she was dressed only in skimpy lingerie, too? She decided to step in. "I was actually checking messages on my cell phone, and the light from the screen hit the fresco at an angle and highlighted the uneven surface."

The reporter gazed up at the ceiling. One cameraman was angled up toward the painting, and another kid was holding some kind of portable light.

"You must have sharp eyes. We have a lot of lights on right now, but it would be pretty dark under here otherwise."

"Well, once I noticed the unevenness, I asked Jack for a flashlight."

"Oh, so he was in here with you at the time?" The reporter flashed her perky gaze on him, a smile twitching at her painted lips.

"Uh..." Jack hesitated and glanced at Vicki.

"Of course. I'm hardly going to go rooting through his house looking for clues without his being present."

She watched Jack's chest fall in relief, which made sadness drift through her. He really didn't want people to think they were an item. Maybe he was already formulating dinner plans for him and Miss Microphone.

"So you came here to the house specifically to look at the map?" The reporter squinted slightly.

The lights and her intense scrutiny made Vicki blink. "Sort of. I was staying with some relatives of Jack's and they got me interested in the family history."

The reporter's eyes brightened and she leaned in. "I've heard some fascinating things about the Drummond family. There's a reward being offered for finding pieces of an old family relic. Is that what you were searching for?"

There was no way out. "Yes." Vicki sagged inwardly. This would only beat more treasure hunters out of the bushes. Although at this point that didn't really matter. She needed to get out of here, reward or no reward. "A chalice, which three brothers brought with them from Scotland. If the three interlocking pieces of the old cup can be reunited, it will bring luck to the family."

"What a romantic story." The reporter smiled at Jack. "Do you believe the cup exists?"

"I don't doubt it. Whether we can find it is a whole other story." He looked relaxed again. "But we're sure having fun looking for it. And Vicki's happy discovery of the treasure map led us to the wreck of my ancestor Macassar Drummond's boat. We've managed to salvage a lot of interesting material from the remains of his ship and have barely scratched the surface. I'd say we have years of rewarding work ahead of us."

"So the lost cup is already bringing you good luck?" Vicki saw the reporter's eyes dart momentarily to his muscled forearm. Of course she thought Jack was hot. Who wouldn't? The poor woman was only human after all.

"That's an interesting way of looking at it. I guess you could say it is bringing us luck." He smiled at Vicki. "And I have my old and dear friend to thank for it."

Vicki cringed inwardly. She didn't much like being described as "old" and "dear." Sounded like she might need a blue rinse or some new knitting patterns. "It's been fascinating for me, too. I'm an art dealer by trade, and interested in historical pieces." She managed a bright smile. Might as well get some decent publicity for herself out of this whole fiasco.

"Really?" Miss Microphone turned her glowing smile on Vicki. "Have you found anything yet that could be described as treasure?"

"We have. I put some pieces aside for you to see."

The reporter made a funny hand gesture that ground everything to a halt. Vicki sagged with relief now that the cameras weren't rolling anymore, and the crew started heaving and trailing their equipment into the other room. Neither she nor Jack moved, so after about two minutes they were left alone in the room, standing right next to the bed.

"This was probably a mistake." He spoke softly and with a hint of humor.

"But an unavoidable one." She had far too much experience with unavoidable mistakes. Climbing into Jack's bed might be her biggest one yet.

"We won't get any peace now."

"Just life in the modern world." She tried to look cooler than she felt.

"This is the first time the modern world has been allowed to intrude into the Drummonds' hideout. Usually it's where I come to get away from all that."

"Then I guess now you know how the rest of us feel. Nowhere to run, nowhere to hide." She shrugged and attempted a casual smile. It failed.

"There's always the open sea." Humor twinkled in his eyes.

"I'm sure your pirate ancestors said the same thing." A smile sneaked to her mouth. It was hard to stay too serious around Jack. Maybe that was part of the problem. Why couldn't she just ask him why he'd gone cold on her? That might make him think their fling actually meant something to her.

And she didn't want him to think that even if it was true.

Better to be glib and casual. "I suppose it's too early in the day for a vodka gimlet." She winced at a loud scraping sound from the other side of the door.

"Not if you're bold enough to drink one on camera."

She blew out. "I'm not as bold as I used to be. Five

years ago I wouldn't have thought twice. Maybe I am getting old and wise."

"You want to watch that. It might get boring."

"Maybe I'm already boring." Again she burned to ask what made him suddenly go off her. The sex had been amazing and Jack wasn't the type to fake an orgasm, even if it was possible for a man to do that.

"You'll never be boring, Vicki St. Cyr."

Then why won't you sleep with me?

The door flung open. "We're ready to start rolling again. We'd love you both to come talk about the stuff you found."

"Sure." She stretched. "I guess the gimlet can wait. God knows I've done crazier things than this stone-cold sober."

Jack laughed, which didn't entirely hide the odd expression in his eyes. If she didn't know better she'd swear he was looking at her with something akin to… tenderness.

But that was impossible. Pirates weren't tender and Jack Drummond was anything but sentimental. "Let's go manhandle the treasure."

It was well after dark by the time the crew finally left, which meant a lengthy and complex process of hauling their equipment back onto their rented boat in the dark. Jack seemed a little on edge, which she wouldn't have believed if she couldn't see it with her own eyes. His shoulders looked tense and a groove had appeared beneath his sun-lightened brows.

The crew had left her careful organization of the boxes and equipment in disarray, and she didn't have the energy to put them back. "When will the story air?"

They'd traded her imaginary vodka gimlet for a glass of chablis, and sipped it while standing in one of the French doors, looking out over the moonlit ocean. Peace had been restored, as long as you were looking outside the windows and not in.

"Tonight, I guess. I don't even know what time the news is on here."

"Don't want to let the outside world intrude on your sanctuary?"

"Not really. I don't watch TV much. I bet you don't, either." He moved close behind her, but not close enough to touch her. "I'm not sure either of us is good at sitting still for long enough to watch a TV show."

Her skin tingled at the feel of him so near...and yet so far. Why couldn't he just touch her, dammit? The wine wasn't helping. It heightened the sensual languor in the warm evening air and filed the edges of her well-honed inhibitions.

Made her long for a long, slow, seductive kiss.

She hugged herself because no one else was going to.

"Cold?"

"No. I guess we should check the TV and see what kind of spin they put on the whole thing." At least if it aired today they wouldn't have time to ferret around in her past. And she couldn't stand still any longer with Jack hovering behind her. Her blood pressure was rising by the second.

"Yeah." He didn't move. And his body blocked the way back into the room. She could feel waves of heat rising off him. Or was that just her fevered imagination?

"Vicki." His voice had an uncharacteristic hesitant tone.

"Yes, I'm Vicki." She immediately cursed herself for

her snarky answer. How could anyone be romantic with her when she was such a prickly sea urchin herself?

"You sure are." He said it softly, then turned and went back into the room, leaving her standing alone on the edge of the darkness. Whatever intimate confession or utterance he'd been about to make would remain forever unspoken.

Fantastic. And she had herself to blame.

She peeled herself away from the door frame, her mind spinning with what Jack might have said. No wonder Leo Parker was the only man in hot pursuit of her right now. A guy would have to be crazy or stupid to chase after someone so difficult. She'd once thought Jack was crazy, but up close he seemed wonderfully sane. Leo was stupid and arrogant—maybe that was the only kind of man who'd ever be interested in her, because everyone else got scared off by her own arrogance and stupidity.

"Are you okay, Vicki? You're breathing a bit funny."

Emotions were welling in her chest. "I'm fine. It's just been a long day."

"You can go to bed if you want. I'll tell you what they say on the news."

She could go off by herself and sleep alone. In Jack Drummond's bed. The thought made her shoulders sag. She'd let some scenarios play through her mind when she decided to come here and look for the cup. Most of them involved Jack trying to get her into bed. Some of them involved her resisting. She'd never even considered the possibility that he'd keep her at a polite but safe distance. "No, thanks. I'll stay up for a while." All night if need be. If the cup was here, she'd find it. If she didn't, she was out of here anyway.

She had to leave or lose her mind. She'd been holding herself together and putting on a brave face for far too long. The promise of a bright future and her own self-confidence had buoyed her along. But now, here, she'd run right out of steam.

She closed the patio door and followed Jack into the den, where a huge sofa wrapped around three walls, so a group of people could stare together at the enormous flat-screen TV on the wall. Someday Jack would watch a football game with his future son in this room, and his yet-to-be-determined wife would probably bring them grilled shrimp and salsa—Jack wasn't really a chips-and-dip guy—and smile fondly at their masculine antics.

And she'd be off somewhere holding a loupe up to an eighteenth-century print to study the paper for foxing. Which was exactly what she wanted.

Jack had settled into the leather sofa, but she held herself against the wall near the door, poised for escape. He clicked past a colorful stream of junky television shows and belligerent commercials, finally settling on the local affiliate whose logo had been all over the house a few hours earlier. The news was under way. "Maybe we missed it." She didn't care much one way or the other. She just needed that cup for her own purposes.

"It won't be the headline story. There's no fresh blood involved, and we're only five minutes into the hour. Maybe it will be the feel-good story at the end."

She hugged herself again, then caught herself doing it and thrust her hands to her sides. She'd have to make her own feel-good story somewhere far away from here.

To keep herself busy, she poured them both a glass

of wine from an open bottle on the sideboard, then held hers untasted, afraid of its intoxicating effects. She already felt emotionally on edge, probably more so than at any time in her life, and the wine might do anything but steady her nerves.

"Here it is!" Jack sat forward as an image of his boat out on the water appeared on the screen to an excited voice-over about the new find. It must have been aerial footage from a helicopter, which cut to the bright gaze of the reporter who'd interviewed them.

"Local resident Jack Drummond has made another thrilling discovery, the sunken wreck of a three-hundred-year-old pirate ship just off our shores. And the best part is, the pirate was his own ancestor, Macassar Drummond."

Jack grinned, enjoying the story as the reporter rattled on about the history of the area and how the Treasure Coast had got its name from the regular encounters between laden ships and tropical storm systems along its palm-fringed shores.

Vicki started at the sight of herself when they cut to a shot inside Jack's house. She looked so serious and less glamorous than she'd imagined, even in her special on-camera getup. Next to Jack, who glowed like a Hollywood star on camera, she seemed small, rather insignificant, prattling on about history and provenance and cataloging techniques. It was a miracle they didn't cut her out altogether, but they did soon switch to some more-engaging footage of Jack on the bow of his boat, wind tossing his hair and the sun beating down on his bronzed skin, every inch the high-seas hero of the popular imagination.

"Well, that was harmless." Jack beamed as they cut

to a commercial and someone started shouting about amazing deals on a new Toyota. "I think we came off as quite a professional operation. Not bad for the scion of notorious pirates."

"It'll still bring all the backyard treasure hunters out of the woodwork."

"Can you blame them? Who wouldn't want in on a haul like this? Now that we've stirred up the silt there'll be coins and clay pipes and musket balls washing up on the beaches for years." He grinned. Obviously he didn't mind one bit that a bunch of strangers would share in the bounty. He was a much more generous and friendly soul than she. No wonder he wanted to cut her loose.

"I'm going to go root through a few more boxes."

"Still looking for that damned cup?" Teasing humor filled his voice.

"Don't come crying to me if you get to live happily ever after because I find it."

"I won't hold my breath. I'm off to bed. We need to get a very early start tomorrow so we can chase off any vultures that start circling."

"Great. See you tomorrow." She'd already left the room and headed down the hallway. She certainly wasn't going to stand around waiting for another embarrassingly polite explanation of why it made more sense for him to sleep in another room.

She switched on the computer and scrolled methodically through the files of X-rays, scrutinizing each one for any shapes that could be either a drinking vessel or a base. A white oval shadow on image number C53 made her pause. Tilted another way, it could be round. Which could mean it was a cup base or even the drinking vessel itself. Well worth investigating.

She rearranged the stacks of boxes to liberate number 53, then pulled out the dripping mass inside it, huge and heavy, and spread it on some damp towels on the floor. Starting with a small chisel and working her way down to a minuscule one, she scraped away the layers of sand and coral and encrusted sea creatures that had taken the strange object into their rock-hard embrace.

As she grew nearer to the mysterious object she'd seen on the X-ray, her blood started to pump harder. She had a real feeling about this thing, and her instincts were nothing to laugh at. People teased her that she could tell a real art object from a fake simply by the way the hairs on her neck stood on end in the presence of greatness, and something about this object was setting off her sixth sense.

If Katherine Drummond's story was true, she could be millimeters away from revealing part of a medieval chalice no one had seen for three hundred years.

It was metal, all right. She tried hard not to scratch the surface as she removed the layers of sandy grit. The silted material fell easily away, revealing the rim of a cup. She bit her lip, afraid to let her hopes soar. The inside of the cup was filled with grit, and she decided to chisel away at the outside first to get some idea of the age before she tackled its contents. Her careful work revealed a delicate etched pattern, emerging almost completely undamaged from its cement overcoat of seabed. And it looked just like the pattern carved on the stem segment they'd found at Sinclair Drummond's Long Island mansion.

I've found it. Elation mingled with unwelcome sadness. Now she could leave. She'd probably never see Jack Drummond again. What a relief. So why was her gut sending up flares of warning?

Ten

Still carrying the weight of its rocky contents, the cup was heavy and large as a man's fist. Vicki wrapped it in a hand towel, ostensibly to protect its surfaces, but mostly to conceal it. She wasn't sure why.

She packed the rest of box 53 away and mopped up the water she spilled, then, clutching the damp towel-wrapped bundle, she headed for the bedroom. She intended to leave without telling Jack. She'd plead exhaustion tomorrow morning and let him go off with the crew, then she'd call for a water taxi and make her way back to civilization.

He'd be none the wiser until he returned that night, by which time she might be safely back in New York, collecting her reward from Katherine Drummond. She'd send Jack his share of the reward once she was safely distant.

She crept along the corridor, praying he wouldn't wake. She didn't want to see him again. It was hurtful and humiliating that she still had feelings for him even after he'd rejected her again. Somehow even the nights alone on cool sheets hadn't chilled the fever of excitement Jack's presence stirred in her blood. If anything, they'd made it worse.

She opened her door gingerly. The old hinges tended to creak and if he was sleeping next door it could wake him up. Not that he'd want to have anything to do with her in the middle of the night. But it would be depressing that he didn't. Better not to have him stir.

She switched on the light, but it hurt her eyes, so she switched it off again. Her big duffel bag was on the dresser, and she unwrapped the cup fragment, then rewrapped it in some flannel pajama bottoms and shoved it deep into her bag. She'd have to remember not to heave it around too enthusiastically tomorrow.

She stripped off her clothes—no need to sleep in any protective armor—and headed for bed. To heck with her makeup; she'd wash it off tomorrow. She climbed up onto the high bed and lifted the covers, ready to climb in and sink down into the soft mattress.

That's when she discovered that the bed was already occupied.

Jack smiled in the dark as Vicki climbed into the bed. The light flicking on had woken him from a deep sleep, and he'd wondered if his sudden appearance back in his own bed might send her running.

She'd hesitated, sure, but then she climbed in and lay still. His skin hummed with awareness, even though no part of her was touching him. His fingers itched to reach out and spread themselves over her hips or around her waist, or to wind their tips into her hair.

But he hesitated. She'd seemed so quiet today, almost vulnerable, different than he'd ever seen her. Was that why he was here? He'd avoided her for two days because he didn't want to give her false hope.

False hope? Who was he to be so arrogant? The only evidence that she wanted a relationship with him at all was her unconscious nighttime ramblings. Maybe she was talking to some other Jack that had nothing to do with him.

An idea that set his nerves on edge.

But now that she seemed so…down, did he think his affectionate arms were the perfect prescription? His reasons for being here suddenly seemed foolish and callous. If she were pining away because he wouldn't sleep with her, wouldn't sleeping with her make that worse instead of better?

He sucked in a silent breath. This was all far too confusing. No wonder his relationships rarely survived the first year. The sea might get rough and unpredictable, but it didn't have hidden motives and inscrutable wishes that could swirl around and suck you under just when you least expected it.

Gingerly, he reached out an exploratory hand. It landed on Vicki's soft thigh. And she didn't slap it away.

He felt her breathing quicken, and his own matched its pace as he eased closer. Her scent heated his blood, intensifying as he buried his face in her hair. Her back was to him, so he bumped gently into the delicious curve of her tight backside, and paused to relish the rush of sensation.

Oh, Vicki.

She hadn't moved at all, but awareness pulsed from every pore. She had every right to play hard to get, after his hot-and-cold behavior of the past few days. His exploratory fingers touched the curve of her breast, and caught the rapid thud of her heart.

She turned toward him oh so slightly, just enough for him to press his lips to her cheek. From there they somehow climbed to her mouth as she rolled over and slipped her arms around him. His chest tightened as she held him, kissing him back.

I love you, Jack. I've always loved you. Her words, unspoken, hovered in his mind. Two phrases, uttered years apart, that had scared him right off. Right now they did nothing to dampen his fierce desire. If anything, they enhanced it.

I love you, too, Vicki. He didn't say it. Instead, he let the thought float in his mind, testing it out. It expanded, filling him with a strange lightness. His body felt good wrapped around hers. This was sheer physical pleasure he was comfortable and familiar with.

But with Vicki, there was always something more. An emotional component that threw him off his game and made him wonder if he was getting in too deep.

Which didn't make any sense, when deep in Vicki was such an awesome place to be.

Their kiss intensified as their hands roamed over each other. When he couldn't stand the building sensation anymore, he entered her. She let out a little whimper of pleasure, nails digging into his skin for an instant before she arched to take him deeper.

He moved over her slowly, floating in the sea of emotions that washed through him. The past two days he'd fought a constant, nagging urge to do just this—

lose himself in her. He'd had plenty to keep him busy, but nothing could keep his mind off her. Those nights alone in the spare bedroom had driven him half-mad. Vicki St. Cyr only a few yards away, wanting him in her bed, and him too…chicken to go there.

He laughed out loud at how ridiculous his behavior had been.

"Why are you laughing?" She breathed faster and faster, and sensation built between them like a wave heading for shore.

"Can't believe how stupid I am," he rasped. "For sleeping alone when we could have been doing this."

"I agree." She whispered the words in his ear, sending a hot sizzle of sensation to his core. "But intelligence never was your strong suit. You're more a man of action."

"True." Trying not to act on his primal instincts to bed Vicki over the past couple of days had half killed him. Finally getting to do what he'd craved all along felt so good he knew he could explode at any minute.

But he didn't. He held himself in check, moving slowly, shifting positions, enjoying the thrill of making Vicki gasp and moan as pleasure shot through her with the same crazy intensity.

Would she say it again? Right now she could say anything and it would sound just right. He and Vicki were meant to be together in some mysterious way. Even during their years apart, something had linked them. A mysterious thread of fate or destiny that had eventually pulled them back together.

"I hope you never find that cup." He breathed the words in between fierce kisses. Her search for the cup had brought her back into his life, and finding it might take her out of it. Right now that was inconceivable.

Her breathing changed slightly, almost like she was holding her breath, and their joint rhythm slowed. She didn't answer. Maybe he was in some realm where speech was no longer possible. That could happen during sex, especially the really good kind like this. He nibbled her ear, then licked it, something that had always driven her crazy.

She whimpered, then wriggled underneath him, inviting him deeper, and they drifted again into that driving rhythm that carried him out where speech, and even thought, became irrelevant. Then they rolled until she was on top and she rode him at a gallop until they both exploded into a climax that left him winded by his own spent passion.

Vicki, Vicki, Vicki. Could he stand to live without her?

Right now the answer was no.

Vicki heard Jack climb out of bed, but kept her eyes closed tight. It was still dark, but she knew he planned to reach the wreck before dawn to beat any treasure seekers who might have seen the news story. She held her breath when she heard him hesitate. Was he wondering whether to sneak out without waking her?

"Vicki, are you coming on the boat today?" That answered one question.

She pretended to half awaken from a groggy sleep. "Too tired."

"Sleep well, gorgeous." She almost opened her eyes when his lips touched hers in a soft kiss. Then she exhaled with relief when she heard the door close behind him.

Memories of last night flooded back, pressing her down into the mattress. Did Jack really have to come sleep with her just because he could? It was humiliating to have so little control around him. She had every excuse to give him the cold shoulder, but apparently even her shoulders couldn't resist him. Thank heavens she'd finally found the cup piece and could get the heck out of here with what little was left of her dignity.

A surge of excitement rushed through her at the thought of the cup. She couldn't wait to bring it to Katherine Drummond, and not just because of the reward. Katherine had placed so much hope in putting the cup back together, and the quest had helped her recover from a dangerous illness. She'd be so excited to hear that the family legend might actually come true.

Vicki stayed rock-still in bed until she heard the distant sound of Jack's boat leaving for the marina to pick up the others. Then she sprang into action. She needed to get out of here before the housekeeper showed up around nine, so she didn't have to answer any awkward questions. She'd already looked up a water taxi service on the internet—cripplingly expensive but she didn't have much choice—and she dialed them. A surprised-sounding man said he could be there in half an hour, and she didn't argue. That would still get her out of here around dawn without seeing Jack.

She showered and attempted to fix her hair in some semblance of a style, then dressed in an all-black ensemble that seemed suited to the somber task of escaping Jack's island.

There was no question of saying goodbye. What if he suggested that she stay awhile longer and she eagerly agreed? What if he waved her off, glad to have his pri-

vate paradise to himself again? There were any number
of possibilities, none of them good. At least this way
she had the advantage of surprise.

She shoved her toiletries into her bag and zipped up
the compartments. What would Jack think when he returned to find her gone? She wanted to feel a thrill of
victory at finally being the one to leave him, but she
didn't. He'd already picked her up and put her down and
played with her like a plastic toy, so there wasn't much
satisfaction in stalking away when he'd already proved
he could do what he liked with her.

And she'd miss him. Maybe that was the worst part.
She'd already missed his joyful energy in her life for
six years. These past few days had reminded her of how
much she enjoyed his company, and the zest and origi-
nality he brought to everything he did. There weren't
too many men around like Jack Drummond.

None, in fact.

But maybe that was a good thing. She shoved her
bag onto her shoulder and slipped her feet into her sandals, then went into the kitchen and made a quick turkey wrap for the road. She didn't have any appetite, so
she shoved the wrap in a ziplock bag and stuck it in an
outside pocket on her bag.

She couldn't resist sneaking a last, long look at the
plastic boxes filled with recovered treasures from the
bottom of the ocean. Seeing them all marinating there
in their seawater gave her another pang of grief. How
much fun would it be to stay here and unwrap each
of them from their sandy giftwrap and watch the past
emerge? Jack was so lucky—and brilliant, really—to
have forged a life doing exactly what he loved. She admired and envied him, and that didn't make leaving

any easier. She should hate him for the way he'd toyed with her, but she couldn't even do that. He was too likable—too lovable—so she'd have to settle for a lifetime of simmering resentment instead.

She wrote a note to Jack as a memo on the computer. At least there the housekeeper wasn't likely to find it and read it.

I'll be back in NYC by the time you read this. I found the cup piece I was looking for and I'll make sure you get half the reward. There's an old Chinese saying that goes "may you live in interesting times" and times are certainly always interesting around you. I think it's supposed to be a curse, so I won't wish for the rest of your life to be interesting because I do wish you all the best. XX Vicki.

Then she decided she'd rambled too much and said the wrong thing and she wanted to delete it, but if she fussed around too much maybe the water taxi wouldn't find the dock and she'd get stuck here trying to explain it in person. She agonized for a moment over what to name the document. *Goodbye* sounded too melodramatic, *Au revoir* implied that she'd see him again, *Laters* sounded too faux-casual, so she went with *Bye, Jack* and turned off the computer.

The sky had lightened somewhat by the time she headed for the dock Jack used for visitors. It was easy to spot from the shore and she raised a colorful flag she'd seen him use to attract the attention of the news crew's boat. Five minutes early, she heard the chugging of an engine, and a battered boat pulled up.

Instead of feeling a great weight lift as the grizzled captain helped her aboard, she felt it settle deeper into the pit of her belly. Once the boat's pilot had turned his attention to steering the boat, she looked back at the lush canopy of palm-topped sea grape that sheltered the infamous Drummond clan from the prying eyes of the outside world. What a magical place. Though Jack probably wouldn't ever find the perfect wife and have the 2.5 towheaded children of his dreams running gaily through the garden. Men like him usually left a trail of broken hearts—and fatherless children—scattered over the globe. For all she knew, he was no different already.

Her broken heart had almost mended from the first time he'd dropped it. This time she might not be so lucky, but never mind. She didn't have much use for a heart anyway.

Back in New York she holed up on her friend Zara's sofa on Prince Street. She could probably stay with Zara for a week on the pretext of looking for a new pad, but because Zara's huge loft was entirely open, the lack of privacy might start to unhinge her after that. She certainly wasn't going back to abuse the hospitality of Sinclair Drummond and his new fiancée. She liked the down-to-earth and practical Annie, and had immediately seen her as a match for Sinclair. But for whatever reason, Annie didn't seem to like her at all.

Sigh.

And there was the awkward reality of having to claim a large reward from a family friend. She'd have to pretend she would donate it to her favorite charity and just not mention that meant herself. Maybe that's why she still hadn't called to tell Katherine about the cup. Determined to get things moving, she picked up her phone and dialed the number.

"Vicki! I was wondering when you'd call. From the news stories I'm seeing, you obviously had no trouble finding Jack."

"Drummonds are easy to find because they stay in the same house for three hundred years."

Katherine laughed. "So true! And you found the cup on the newly discovered wreck?"

"It's a long story." She arranged to come out to Long Island and visit Katherine the next day. She would have been totally ashamed to admit that her chief motivation was to get her hot little hands on the twenty-thousand-dollar check. And she might not be in too much of a rush to get Jack's share to him. With all his millions he wouldn't mind waiting a month or so.

She took the train out to Long Island to avoid the expense of renting a car, and wasn't surprised when Annie met her at the station. Vicki greeted her with a friendly wave. "I see you're still the most helpful person in Dog Harbor."

Once again, Annie stiffened. She tried to take Vicki's bag and put it in the trunk. Vicki held on tight. "I can handle it. You're no stronger than me and you're not the housekeeper anymore."

"Did you have a good train ride?" Annie asked primly.

"No worse than usual. Annie, can I ask you to be completely frank with me?" She settled into the passenger seat.

"Okay." Annie looked anything but enthusiastic as she reversed out of the parking space.

"I can tell you don't like me, and I'm just wondering why." She looked at Annie, whose pretty, almost-strawberry-blond hair was loose to her shoulders for once.

Annie turned to her with a look that could only be described as distressed. "For one thing, I never know what you're going to say. And when you do say something, it usually throws me off guard. Frankly, you scare me a little." Annie's words had rushed out in one breath. She then realized that she'd reversed out and was blocking the street, and she swung the car around into the right lane.

"Oh." Vicki drew in a breath. "I'm sorry." She felt chastened. She didn't tend to worry all that much about other people's feelings. Maybe because she wasn't the world's most sensitive person herself. Often she didn't even notice when someone disliked her until someone else pointed it out. Even then, she usually didn't mind too much.

But somehow she wanted Annie to like her, and it hurt that she didn't.

"And you know what?" Annie continued, a slight frown marring her smooth brow. "It was weird being the housekeeper and waiting on people hand and foot. I had to be polite to everyone whether I wanted to or not. It's kind of stressful."

"And now you can be as rude as you like." Vicki raised a brow.

Annie laughed. "I don't think I'm capable of that. I'm too repressed or something. I think you and I are just opposites."

"Which is why I'd be disastrous with the lovely Sinclair and you're his perfect match. I could see it from the first moment I saw you together."

"How?" Annie sounded genuinely curious. "I didn't think we were all right for each other. I doubt we would ever have got together if you hadn't forced us into it."

Vicki looked sideways at her. "You can't fool me. Something had already happened between you."

Annie bit her lip. "Something…totally wild and unexpected and inappropriate and, well, eek!"

"And now it's turned into something wonderful and perfect and joyous for all concerned."

"And I have to give you credit where credit's due. I think I do like you after all." Annie smiled at her.

"I'm not even sure if I like myself." Vicki stared out the windshield. "Maybe I'll grow on both of us."

Katherine Drummond's pale eyes filled with tears at the sight of the cup. Still weak from a rare tropical illness, she sat in a polished chair at the dining table in her son's Long Island mansion. Sinclair stood nearby with his arm around his fiancée, Annie, and all attention was riveted on the artifact Vicki had pulled from her bag.

Tarnished and still somewhat encrusted with seabed, the cup didn't look at all impressive. Suddenly Vicki even wondered if it was the right cup. Maybe the pieces wouldn't fit together and her time would have all been wasted.

"Vicki, darling, I can't believe you went to such lengths to find this."

"It was all Jack's doing."

"How did you talk him into looking for it? I couldn't even get him to return my calls."

"I just had to fire up his treasure hunting instincts. It really wasn't hard. Shouldn't we make sure it fits?"

Katherine reached for the unimpressive-looking stem that sat in a fabric-lined box on the table in front of her. She squeezed it in her bony hand and looked at Vicki. "I know we still have to find the third piece, but I can't help but feel a sense of history being made right at this moment."

Vicki held her breath. How disappointed would she be if this was all a big mistake? Katherine hoped to end the Drummond family's long run of disastrous marriages and personal tragedies with this battered relic. That was a lot of hope to hang on one old cup.

She held out the cup and Katherine pushed the stem into the hole on the underside of the cup bowl. There was a grinding noise as remaining encrusted sand and mineral deposits scraped against metal. Vicki wished she'd taken the time to clean it more thoroughly, but she'd been impatient to come here and claim the reward.

"It fits." Katherine looked up at Vicki, tears glittering in her eyes. "Look, Sinclair." She held it up like a priest during Mass. "The legend is real!"

Sinclair raised an eyebrow. "Pretty cool."

Vicki wanted to laugh. Sinclair was so not the type to get fired up over a crusty old antique. His future wife wasn't, either. They were all wrapped up in plans for Annie to open a shop selling decorative home and garden items. Neither of them was at all worried about the impact of ancient curses and legends on their future.

Katherine twisted the cup in the light. "I wonder if you're supposed to drink a libation out of it?"

"I think you should wait until you find the third piece." Vicki stared at the cup, which visibly lacked its base. "Have you had any luck contacting the Scottish branch of the family?"

Katherine shook her head. "None whatsoever. It's very frustrating. I would be upset with James Drummond for being so rude, but apparently he spends most of his time in Singapore, so I'm not even sure that his Scottish estate is passing along my messages. I don't suppose you'd be willing to go there and track him down, Vicki?"

Vicki froze. "No, I'm afraid I really have to get back to my life in New York." The last thing she needed was to meet another tall, dark and debonair Drummond heir. They were all bad news as far as she was concerned. "Maybe you should visit him yourself?"

"The doctors won't let me travel. My immune system took such a beating they're worried that even a bad cold could knock me flat, so no air travel." She rolled her eyes. "I guess I'll just have to keep phoning and emailing James Drummond. Sooner or later I'll get through to him." Katherine turned the cup in her hands again. "But I feel a weight lifting already. I know we'll find the third piece. Look how happy Sinclair is." She glanced fondly at her tall, imposing son, who did glow rather sweetly with happiness.

Vicki felt even her hard heart swell with emotion. "I'm sure you will and I can't wait to see it all together. In the meantime, however, I'm afraid I must run. I wanted to bring you the piece I found as soon as possible, but I've been on vacation from my life for some weeks and I have a lot to do." She swallowed, hoping she wouldn't have to remind Katherine about the reward. She'd managed to conceal her lack of money all this time, but things were getting desperate. Her credit cards were maxed out and she needed to pay them down to get herself off the ground in New York.

"It seems rather a shame that the reward you talked me into offering is going to people who already have money." Katherine laughed. "I suppose you can always give it to the needy."

Vicki managed a fake laugh. "Of course. I have some pet causes." Like eating and having a roof over her head. "And I'm sure Jack does, too."

"I saw the two of you on the news. I couldn't help but notice that you'd make a lovely couple."

"How odd it made the news here." Vicki's swallowed. Her fling was supposed to be private and personal. Would others guess there was something between them? "I thought it was a local interest story."

"It's one of the biggest finds of the century. It's nice to see the Drummonds getting good publicity for a change. Usually we're only in the papers when someone crashes their plane into a building or disappears at sea. Jack is very dashing. Don't you think he's handsome?"

"I guess." Adrenaline surged through her. Could she just beg Katherine to write the check? "Kind of arrogant, but why wouldn't he be?"

"Why not indeed." Katherine smiled fondly. "Maybe he'll find love now that the cup is being reunited."

Vicki felt ill. "Goodness, look at the time. A check would be great."

Subletting a studio on Sutton Place was a coup. She chose the tony address entirely for the snob factor. Although her building was right on the East River, her tiny apartment was on the first floor and faced toward the street. Still, it made for great letterhead and she could walk down to the water and sip coffee looking out at Roosevelt Island whenever she wanted.

Writing a check for ten thousand dollars and mailing it to Jack Drummond didn't feel quite so hot. She'd hoped that once she posted it she could put that whole unfortunate episode of her life behind her. Then she found herself obsessively checking her bank balance—never a good thing to do—to see if he'd cashed it. And he didn't.

Did the check go astray? Was he too busy to visit an ATM machine? Did he suspect she needed the money and decide to treat her as a charity case? The possibilities danced in her brain even as she hustled to get her new business off the ground.

She hooked up with her first two clients through an interior decorator she'd met at a party. The first was a Brazilian shoe manufacturer who had a new Park Avenue pad with empty walls and needed to amass a lifetime's art collection in time for his daughter's engagement party in six weeks. The second was an advertising art director who'd just inherited several million and bought a Tribeca loft, and wanted to fill the space with contemporary masters. Could life get any better than that? She had plenty to do, calling around her contacts and attending auctions with an enormous budget to buy anything from Renoir sketches to Rikrit Tiravanija sculptures. With the commissions she'd already started to earn she'd be back in the black and on her way to financial stability by the end of the year.

Life was good. Except for that nagging hole that nothing seemed to fill. Sex didn't work, even with the delicious David from Sotheby's. The unfortunate truth that she craved a more substantial relationship really depressed her when she allowed herself to think about it. So she didn't.

Nearly a month had gone by since she'd returned. Should she call to see if the check got lost? Every time she picked up the phone, her heart beat so fast she wasn't sure she could sound normal, so she put it back down. Sometimes she jumped when her phone rang because she was so sure it must be Jack, calling to cuss her out for taking off without even showing him his own ancestral relic. But he obviously didn't care much one way or the other.

Then one night, the bleat of her phone startled her from her laptop, where she'd been perusing listings for an upcoming Christie's auction. It was him. This time she was sure.

"Hello." She cursed her hopeful tone.

"Vicki." A male voice, but not Jack's. "It's Leo."

Ugh. Her heart sank. "Hi." No encouragement. She'd love to hang up on him, but he was a bit too well connected for overt rudeness.

"When's the wedding?"

"The what?" She smacked her head when she remembered her pretend engagement ruse.

"You're not with Jack Drummond anymore, are you?" His voice had an edge to it that she didn't remember hearing before. He'd probably figured out she was lying. Especially if he'd seen the TV coverage.

"No. No, we broke up." Or were never together in the first place. "I have a call coming in on the other line. Can I call you back?"

"You won't call me back. You've never called me back."

Maybe you could take a hint from that. "Why did you

call?" Might as well get this over with properly. She'd be bound to run into Leo soon because they moved in the same circles, and a pointed conversation now could save an embarrassing scene later.

"I'm sorry it didn't work out with Jack Drummond, but now that you're single again, we could see *La Traviata* and grab dinner at Per Se."

This guy was scary. "I'm still in love with Jack." As she said the words, she knew they were true.

"He's an oaf."

"He's wonderful." Was she really having this conversation?

"Then why did you break up with him?"

"I didn't. He broke up with me." Now, that was the first lie of the conversation, except about the call coming in. Mercifully Jack never had the chance to dump her because she'd taken the reins of that carriage. Of course it had the unfortunate effect of leaving her wondering what might have happened if…

"Listen, Vicki. I've been very patient with you, but you're taxing even my vast reserves. I want to take you to dinner, and you *will* come."

"I won't." All this talk about Jack made her feel reckless.

"Don't forget that I know about your family's financial trouble. How would you like for me to go to the papers with that news?"

"Go right ahead." And she pressed End. Then blew out a long, hard breath. *Do your worst, Leo Parker.* She couldn't live with threats and secrets hanging over her head. She was good at what she did. So what if her ivory tower was in foreclosure? People would just have to take her as they found her.

* * *

The story broke slowly over the next week. A gossip column mention here, a blog there, an opinion piece about privilege and greed…and the results were disastrous. Her two clients ran in separate directions, leaving her holding the checks for three artworks she'd already purchased as the only salvage from her brief career as art buyer to the rich and famous. She retreated to her Sutton Place lair to lick her wounds and wait for the firestorm of gossip to die down.

"No one will even remember in a month." Annie had called to commiserate after seeing a story on *The Huffington Post*. "These things get people all excited and then they move on to some other new drama."

"I'm surprised anyone cares, but I suppose I knew they would, which is why I hid the truth for so long. Poverty is terrifying to the rich."

Annie laughed. "You're hardly impoverished."

"That's what you think." It was a relief to be honest. "I'm just good at keeping up appearances. I've been living from hand to mouth for nearly a year. Why do you think I spent so much time mooching around you and Sinclair?"

"I thought you liked us. I should have known better. What are you going to do?"

"I'll survive. What doesn't kill me, and all that jazz. Maybe I'll travel to Scotland in hopes of earning the rest of the reward."

"Really?"

"No." A banging noise made her jump. "I'd better go. Someone's at the door." That was odd. The doorman usually buzzed and announced anyone who turned up. She said goodbye and put down her phone.

Her gut flared with warning. Could Leo Parker have come around to up the ante? He was obviously crazy and vindictive and out to get her where it hurt. "Who is it?"

"It's Jack."

Eleven

She opened the door and stood there like a mute for about thirty seconds. Jack Drummond in her doorway was not a possibility that had ever crossed her mind. "How did you find me?"

"I'm a treasure hunter." A wicked grin was already creeping across his mouth. His dark eyes sparkled with pleasure and he looked as if he was enjoying himself. "If it's worth finding, I'll find it."

She cursed the way her body already responded to his presence, prickling with awareness. "Why?"

"First, to tell you I don't want any part of the reward." He came in and shut the door behind him without asking.

"But you—" She wasn't sure what to protest about first: his refusing the reward or barging into her apartment. Being in close proximity to Jack was dangerous.

"Don't say it." He held up his hand. "I know you're short of cash, and you know I'm not."

Ouch. He pitied her. That was even harder to take than his pushing her out of his bed. Her skin crawled with humiliation. "I'm fine." Her protest seemed foolish now that everyone in the world knew her financial predicament. It was automatic, like a twitch. "And you need to leave."

Not a single muscle moved beneath his white T-shirt or the faded jeans that hugged his powerful legs. The worst part was how badly she wanted to rush into his arms and throw herself against that hard chest.

It took great effort to stand her ground. "Jack, I don't know what you're up to, but there's no good reason for you to be here and—"

"No good reason? You sneaked off with my family heirloom. I never even got a chance to see it." The mischievous gleam in his eyes belied his supposed anger.

"You never cared about that cup. Besides, I don't have it. I gave it to Katherine."

He sighed. "I know. I've just come from a touching reunion with that branch of the family. Sinclair and Annie do make a cute couple and I hear that you played millionaire matchmaker for them."

"At least I've done something right this year." Could she forcibly push him out the door? She was afraid of what might happen if she pressed her palms against his contoured pecs. Already the temperature in the room had shot up ten degrees.

"I miss you, Vicki." He spoke directly, no teasing humor. "I was happy until you came to visit."

"And I ruined everything. Story of my life." She threw up her hands, babbling, anything to break the tension in the air. "I have a knack for making people uncomfortable." She thrust her hands on her hips. Emotion built inside her, all the pent-up hurt and frustrated affection she'd never gotten to express. She'd been nervous about seeing Jack when she went down to Florida, and with good reason. She'd thought she could handle herself around him, and she'd been wrong. This time he'd left a wound too large and raw to heal. "You really have to leave."

"I'm not going anywhere." He stood there in the tiny foyer of her tiny apartment, looming like a colossus. "Why did you run off?"

"This is my apartment. I think I should have some say in who enters it." She crossed her arms over her chest, where her heart was slamming against her rib cage. "And I didn't run off. I simply left."

"Without telling me."

"I didn't want a scene." She lifted her chin.

"And you thought I'd make one?" Humor glinted in his eyes, sparking both fury and defeat in her chest.

"Maybe I was afraid you wouldn't make one." She shrugged. "I never should have slept with you again. It was a big mistake."

"It wasn't." He spoke softly, but his words grew to fill the whole apartment. "I thought it was at first. That I'd gotten in over my head. That's why I pulled back and went to sleep in the other room." He looked sheepish. "That's the only mistake that was made. I was an idiot and I apologize. I never wanted to sleep anywhere but right next to you."

Vicki trembled. Jack Drummond apologizing? Something very strange was going on. "Then why did you do it? Sleep in the other room, I mean." Curiosity overwhelmed her sense of self-preservation.

Jack hesitated. "You said something in your sleep that scared me."

"Was I muttering about sharp knives and revenge?" She lifted her chin. Embarrassing possibilities swirled in her mind.

He tilted his head slightly and looked at her through narrowed eyes. "You said you loved me."

Heat flooded her face. "You must have heard wrong." She'd said that six years ago, sure, but she'd rather cut out her tongue than make the same idiotic mistake twice.

He shook his head. "Clear as a bell. You weren't awake and I'm sure you didn't mean for me to hear it." He frowned. "You said you'd always loved me. It spooked the heck out of me."

"I'll bet. What a nightmare." She fought the urge to throw open the living room window and dive out. Had Jack come here to toy with her? A red-hot tide of pain and humiliation was rising to flood levels inside her. "And you came back here in hopes that you could have a good laugh over it with me?"

"No." He stepped forward, unfamiliar frustration written on his bold features. "I came here because I realized that I...I..." His brow creased. "I love you, too."

Vicki's jaw dropped. The words had emerged from his mouth slowly, deliberately, as though he really meant them. They echoed in her heart, but she still didn't believe them. "Are you messing with me because I didn't say goodbye nicely?" She cocked her head, sure he was going to start laughing any moment.

"I'm not good at this. I've had no practice. I'm the

descendant of scurvy pirates and my genetic heritage is telling me to throw you over my shoulder and head for the high seas. I'm miserable without you and I don't want to be miserable."

The intense expression in his brown eyes surprised her so much that she almost wanted to laugh, maybe just to relieve the tension crackling in the air like an electric storm.

She had no idea what to say. Thoughts whirled in her mind. Jack loved her. He'd come to New York to find her. He wanted to take her away with him. Could this be real?

"I want you to come back to my island. The whole place seems empty without you. Even my boat feels like something's missing."

"I don't belong there." She was trying to convince herself. She'd missed that cursed island every minute since she left it. And his big rambling house with its funky piratical layout. And the comfortable bed where his ancestors had slept under their treasure map. "I'm a New York girl at heart, and you know it." Would he believe it? She didn't. Still, he didn't mean this. Maybe he was just so pissed that she'd finally got the better of him that he thought he loved and needed her. If she said yes and came back with him, he'd tire of her once the thrill of victory wore off.

Jack took another step forward. "I don't think you are a New York girl at heart. I think you love adventure and discovery. You took to the water like a fish, and I know you enjoyed exploring the wreck and unwrapping all its treasures."

She shrugged. "Sure." It was hard to sound casual with her heart smashing against her ribs and emotion clawing at her throat. "But that doesn't mean I'm meant to throw up my whole life and run after you. I just started my own business." *Never mind that it's dried right up already.* "I need to get back on my feet and figure out what I really want."

It didn't matter if what she really wanted was Jack. She'd already learned—twice—how well that worked out for her.

Jack's muscles tightened. Probably unaccustomed frustration at not getting his way. He took a step forward and grabbed her hands. Emotion flashed through her, along with the physical sensation of his touching her skin. She struggled to hold herself steady and keep her expression neutral.

"I love you, dammit. I can't live without you. I want you to be my wife."

She couldn't move. He wanted to marry her? She couldn't imagine Jack married to anyone. "Have you lost your mind?"

"Apparently, yes. And there's only one way to get it back." Still clutching her hands, he dropped onto one denim-clad knee. "Vicki St. Cyr, will you marry me?"

She stared at him. "I must be dreaming. Or hallucinating. Maybe I have a high fever and have temporarily gone insane."

"That makes two of us, then." His chest rose and fell as he looked up at her. "I won't take no for an answer. You know we're perfect for each other."

"No one else could stand us." The sheer madness of the idea made it seem strangely logical. A smile struggled to cross her mouth.

"I love you, Vicki. I think I've loved you since I first met you. I was just too cowardly to admit it. I'm stronger now, and braver, and I've come to claim you." He squeezed her hands and stood up.

Eye to eye with him she suddenly felt weak, as though she could fall into his strong arms and rest there. Tears rose in her eyes and she fought to keep them from spilling. "I do love you, Jack. I have always loved you, although most of the time I've hated myself for it. I certainly didn't intend for you to find out."

His face brightened. "I'm glad I did. It knocked some sense into me. You know we need each other, don't you?"

She nodded. Then swallowed. "But we're both free spirits, Jack. That's why it's never worked out for us before." Mostly she was worried about his free spirit wanting to tack off into a headwind, leaving her behind, but it sounded less pathetic if she blamed herself, too.

"We can be free spirits together." His chest rose. "Why not? If you want to be in New York, then I can spend time here, too. It's easy enough to fly—or sail—back and forth. Then on weekends we can cruise to Madagascar or Brazil."

She laughed, finally, which released a huge bubble of tension. "That sounds so crazy and stupid that it actually makes sense." Her hands felt hot inside his. She longed to free them and grab hold of him. As if he'd heard her thoughts, he let go of her hands and wrapped his arms around her. The breath flew from her lungs as she grabbed him around his huge chest. "Oh, Jack, we're doomed, aren't we?"

"Yup. We'll just have to strap ourselves together like shipwreck survivors and hope for the best."

He pressed her cheek to his shoulder, mostly so she could get away from his fierce gaze. "I do love your island. It makes a good base for adventures." Already her mind was wrapping itself around this strange and wonderful new set of possibilities. "And it would be a fun place for children to grow up."

The silence was deafening. Had she really just said that?

"I'm not going to pressure you into having children. Any big decisions, we'll make together."

"We'd probably have to homeschool them." She lifted her head and found herself frowning at him. "Or we'd be stuck with someone else's schedule."

He nodded, eyes shining with emotion. "Whatever we do, I know it will be an adventure."

Their lips finally met and a tidal wave of relief crashed over her, mingled with the sharp excitement of kissing Jack.

His throaty groan suggested that he felt the same way. When they finally pulled apart enough to speak, he kept his strong arms locked around her waist. "I came to your bed that last night because I finally realized I was an idiot to waste one more night away from the woman I love."

Her heart squeezed. "You must have been pretty pissed when you saw my note the next morning."

"Poleaxed is a better *p* word for the way I felt. My first instinct was to run after you and drag you back, but my pride prevented me. Eventually it wore off." His rakish grin made her smile. "So here I am. I thoroughly deserved to be dumped and abandoned by you, and I promise I'll spend the rest of my life making it up to you."

"Sounds like a plan."

Epilogue

Six months later

"I'm amazed at how much insurance premiums drop when you tell them you're keeping the insured item on a private island." Vicki took a few steps back to get a better look at the pretty little Vermeer she'd picked up in Brugge. At least she was convinced it was a Vermeer. The gallery owner had attributed it to a minor Dutch painter, but it had a certain *je ne sais quoi,* and she was pretty sure she could convince the art world she'd found a lost painting by the revered master.

Jack lay on the big leather sofa, holding up a heavy and time-darkened musket. "Insurance. Now there's a concept."

"You don't keep any?"

"Don't have to when the stuff's all mine." He flashed

his pearly pirate grin. "And my reputation is my insurance. Everyone knows I collect muskets."

"And cannons."

"And cannon balls. And powder." He laughed. "But the stuff you bring home is prettier."

"Isn't she?" The picture showed a young woman, wearing not a pearl earring, but a tiny gold locket. She wondered what secret her locket held. A lock of her beloved's hair? A love note? Or maybe she was just getting soft in her old age. "I can't wait to find her a loving home. Preferably a very rich one."

He laughed. "I love your mercenary streak. Especially because it brought you back into my life."

"I donated Katherine's twenty-thousand-dollar reward to charity. I felt it was the right thing to do now that I'm back on my feet." She pointed to her red Ferragamo sandals.

"And such lovely feet they are. What charity did you pick?"

"A fund for starving artists, of course. Got to keep the pool of talent humming." She smiled. It felt so good to have money to give away again. Or just to have fun with. The shipwreck treasure was still being removed and cleaned and would bring in millions over the next few years. "Where are we going next?"

"That depends on what we're looking for—an old wreck or a valuable painting."

She lifted a brow. "Or a valuable painting disguised as an old wreck by the passage of time."

"We've had such good luck finding both already that it's hard to decide. Did they ever hear from the Scottish Drummond who supposedly has the base of the cup?"

"Not a word last I heard. He's some financial bigwig who spends all his time in Singapore."

"I'd have thought Cousin Sinclair might be able to launch an appeal to a fellow money man."

"I don't think Sinclair is all that interested. Those financial types don't appreciate quirky treasures and their mysteries the way you and I do."

"True. And as far as I know, James Drummond is still single. Finding his third of the cup could spell the end of that."

She laughed. "Maybe that's why he doesn't want any part of it."

Jack put down his musket and strode across the room. He slid his arms around her in that deliciously proprietary way that still made her gasp with excitement. "He doesn't know what he's missing."

"I don't suppose anyone does until love blindsides them when they least expect it." She ran her thumb over his rough cheek. "I certainly didn't think I'd fall madly in love again. Especially with the same man who broke my tender young heart."

"Lucky for me you're rash and impetuous enough to make the same mistake twice." He kissed her lips, sending a shiver of pleasure through her. "I love a woman who isn't afraid to wade into trouble."

"How do you do that to me?" She writhed as he nibbled her earlobe, sending shock waves of arousal dancing through her.

"I'm a keen student of your erogenous zones." He touched a thumb to her nipple through her thin blouse. It immediately thickened under the pressure. "I'm drawing a mental treasure map of them."

"That will lead you right to where X marks the spot?"

"Oh, I already know where that is." He growled softly in her ear, sending a rush of heat to her groin. "Let's go explore it right now."

Together they ran down the corridor, bare feet noiseless on the stone flags, and climbed onto the ancient carved bed where they'd spend countless nights making love under the secret map they'd found together.

* * * * *

COMING NEXT MONTH from Harlequin Desire®
AVAILABLE JANUARY 2, 2013

#2203 ALL OR NOTHING
The Alpha Brotherhood
Catherine Mann
Casino magnate Conrad Hughes wrecked his marriage with his secret work with Interpol. Three years later, this hero has a chance to win back his wife—if he can keep her safe.

#2204 A CONFLICT OF INTEREST
Daughters of Power: The Capital
Barbara Dunlop
A White House PR specialist finds her personal and professional lives in conflict when she becomes pregnant with a newsman's baby as scandal threatens the president.

#2205 SUNSET SURRENDER
Rich, Rugged Ranchers
Charlene Sands
The one woman Logan Slade hoped never to see again is back—and suddenly memories of a stolen teenage kiss thwart Logan's firm resolve to keep his nemesis at arm's length.

#2206 ALL GROWN UP
The Men of Wolff Mountain
Janice Maynard
After being rebuffed as a young woman, Annalise Wolff acts as if she hates Sam Ely. But when they get snowed in on the job, the sparks fly!

#2207 UNDENIABLE DEMANDS
Secrets of Eden
Andrea Laurence
Wade Mitchell is desperate to regain the trust of an architect he once fired, and to reclaim the property she now owns—which holds secrets about his past.

#2208 IN HIS BROTHER'S PLACE
Elizabeth Lane
When Jordan Cooper takes in his late twin brother's son, he falls in love with the boy's mother. But will a tragic secret destroy their future?

You can find more information on upcoming Harlequin®
titles, free excerpts and more at www.Harlequin.com.

HDCNM1212

REQUEST YOUR FREE BOOKS!
2 FREE NOVELS PLUS 2 FREE GIFTS!

Harlequin® *Desire*

ALWAYS POWERFUL, PASSIONATE AND PROVOCATIVE

YES! Please send me 2 FREE Harlequin Desire® novels and my 2 FREE gifts (gifts are worth about $10). After receiving them, if I don't wish to receive any more books, I can return the shipping statement marked "cancel." If I don't cancel, I will receive 6 brand-new novels every month and be billed just $4.30 per book in the U.S. or $4.99 per book in Canada. That's a saving of at least 14% off the cover price! It's quite a bargain! Shipping and handling is just 50¢ per book in the U.S. and 75¢ per book in Canada.* I understand that accepting the 2 free books and gifts places me under no obligation to buy anything. I can always return a shipment and cancel at any time. Even if I never buy another book, the two free books and gifts are mine to keep forever.

225/326 HDN FEF3

Name	(PLEASE PRINT)	
Address		Apt. #
City	State/Prov.	Zip/Postal Code

Signature (if under 18, a parent or guardian must sign)

Mail to the **Reader Service:**
IN U.S.A.: P.O. Box 1867, Buffalo, NY 14240-1867
IN CANADA: P.O. Box 609, Fort Erie, Ontario L2A 5X3

Not valid for current subscribers to Harlequin Desire books.

Want to try two free books from another line?
Call 1-800-873-8635 or visit www.ReaderService.com.

* Terms and prices subject to change without notice. Prices do not include applicable taxes. Sales tax applicable in N.Y. Canadian residents will be charged applicable taxes. Offer not valid in Quebec. This offer is limited to one order per household. All orders subject to credit approval. Credit or debit balances in a customer's account(s) may be offset by any other outstanding balance owed by or to the customer. Please allow 4 to 6 weeks for delivery. Offer available while quantities last.

Your Privacy—The Reader Service is committed to protecting your privacy. Our Privacy Policy is available online at www.ReaderService.com or upon request from the Reader Service.

We make a portion of our mailing list available to reputable third parties that offer products we believe may interest you. If you prefer that we not exchange your name with third parties, or if you wish to clarify or modify your communication preferences, please visit us at www.ReaderService.com/consumerschoice or write to us at Reader Service Preference Service, P.O. Box 9062, Buffalo, NY 14269. Include your complete name and address.